TWICE TEMPTED BY THE PRINCESS

NINA MILNE

ROMANCE

Recycling programs for this product may not exist in your area.

ISBN-13: 978-1-335-21703-5

Twice Tempted by the Princess

For questions and comments about the quality of this book, please contact us at CustomerService@Harlequin.com.

Harlequin Enterprises ULC
22 Adelaide St. West, 41st Floor
Toronto, Ontario M5H 4E3, Canada
www.Harlequin.com

HarperCollins Publishers
Macken House, 39/40 Mayor Street Upper,
Dublin 1, D01 C9W8, Ireland
www.HarperCollins.com

Printed in U.S.A.

1 2 3 4 5 6 7 8 9 10 HDC 28 27 26 25

Long-Lost Rossi Siblings

Hearts entwine among the vines...

The Rossis have owned their billion-dollar Tuscan vineyard for centuries. But since tragedy befell the family, Amara and her grandfather have been left to run the Rossi Estate alone. Until they discover the existence of twins Lorenzo and Daisy—Amara's long-lost half-siblings!

The legacy buried in the estate's soil binds them. Yet, as their family secrets are uncorked, the Rossi siblings find themselves going in three different directions, each of them unknowingly heading straight toward their perfect pairing... But, after childhoods marred by loss and mistreatment, opening their hearts isn't easy. Love is the most intoxicating vintage—will they be brave enough to take a sip? Find out in...

Amara and Gio's story...
The Bride Wore His Convenient Ring

Lorenzo and Liyana's story...
Twice Tempted by the Princess

Both available now!

And don't miss Daisy's story

Coming soon!

Dear Reader,

For me this book is about the idea of being able to trust in love. Unfortunately for me, it became clear that neither Lorenzo or Liyana agreed with that idea at all, and there were times when I despaired of them ever finding a route to the happy ending I hope you agree they deserve. However, I persevered, and amid sun and sand and storms, love does find a way.

I hope you enjoy finding out how.

Nina x

Nina Milne has always dreamed of writing for Harlequin Romance—ever since she played libraries with her mother's stacks of Harlequin romances as a child. On her way to this dream, Nina acquired an English degree, a hero of her own, three gorgeous children and—somehow!—an accountancy qualification. She lives in Brighton and has filled her house with stacks of books—her very own *real* library.

Books by Nina Milne

Harlequin Romance

The Christmas Pact

Snowbound Reunion in Japan

Royal Sarala Weddings

His Princess on Paper
Bound by Their Royal Baby

Winter Escapes

Cinderella's Moroccan Midnight Kiss

Summer Escapes

Their Mauritius Wedding Ruse

Princesses of Palosia

Secret Royal's Napoli Reunion

Long-Lost Rossi Siblings

The Bride Wore His Convenient Ring

Consequençe of Their Dubai Night
Wedding Planner's Deal with the CEO

Visit the Author Profile page
at Harlequin.com for more titles.

To Elina and Aga and all their care

PROLOGUE

Seven years ago

PRINCESS LIYANA OF CARATHI entered the grandiose portals of the discreet yet luxurious London hotel, headed across the black and white marbled floor of the lobby and stood unobtrusively to one side, behind an immense verdant potted plant. Glancing round, she absorbed a décor that rivalled the Grand Palace on Carathi: crystal chandeliers hung from ceilings decorated with gold inlay, gold and black wrought-iron doors and balustrades demarcated the next floor up and the expansive lobby was dotted with red brocaded chairs and spotless glass-topped mahogany tables. Turning to look at the majestic sweep of stairs, she saw her brother head down towards the lobby and congratulated herself on her timing.

Heading towards him, she handed over the

helium ballon with the number 21 emblazoned on it. 'Happy birthday, big bro.'

'Thank you, Nangi.' Prince Ashan used the familiar word for little sister as he took the offering, then studied his sister with a look of perplexion as Liyana attempted a beaming smile.

'You look surprised to see me.'

'I am surprised to see you. Because you've *already* wished me happy birthday. A few hours ago, when we met for a celebratory lunch.' Ashan's eyes narrowed as he surveyed her, no doubt taking in the elegant high-necked long black dress that fell in modest folds to her ankles, the gauze shawl that fell to cover her arms with decorum. Discreet make-up, hair pulled up in an elaborate bun that allowed a few tendrils to frame her face. Party dress Carathi style and Liyana was proud of the effort.

She nodded, met his gaze full on, tried to keep her tone light and persuasive. 'And over the smoked salmon starter you told me that you were planning to celebrate in "style" with your friends tonight and for the next two days. That got me thinking. Why can't I come along too? Just for an hour or two? We're friends, aren't we?'

'Yes, we are. But you are also my sister and I have no intention of taking you with me. I can't, Lili, you know that.'

'But no one will even know it's me,' Liyana pointed out. 'I can blend in for a short time. A couple of cocktails and then I'll go. You can say I'm a friend from home or a staff member or…anything you want.' The chances of recognition were minimal: the small kingdom off the coast of Sri Lanka was not well known and in addition, as a Carathian princess, she led an incredibly sheltered life. Until she reached the age of twenty-two, in two years' time, she wasn't even allowed to carry out public duties; instead, she was expected to study and prepare for her life ahead, kept out of the public eye.

Ashan shook his head. 'Amma and Papa would be horrified if I let you come. And if any pictures end up on social media, *they* will recognise you. I anticipate this is going to be a bit of a wild night and—'

'I'm a girl, so no wild nights allowed. It's not fair.' Liyana knew she sounded like a petulant child, but she *felt* petulant.

'You're a princess,' Ashan said. 'You know the rules. Our kingdom, our people, our family have expectations of royalty and the golden rule is no scandal at all. And princesses have to follow the etiquette set out in our culture. I am sorry but I can't, I won't, take you with us.'

Liyana knew he meant it. The unwritten rules dictated it was OK for a prince to sow a few wild oats as long as he was also dedicated to duty. Which Ashan was. He loved his country and he took his duty to his people, to the island of Carathi, seriously. In a few years he would settle down, marry and produce the heirs that were so vital to the monarchy.

And Liyana too would do her duty, knew that one day she too would make a political marriage, forge an alliance that would help her country. But somehow this year in London, where she was doing a foundation degree, felt like a taste of a freedom she could never have at home.

She knew her parents had had grave reservations about the idea of Liyana spending time in London. Had only agreed because they believed it would be good for the future of the island if the royal family had more experience and knowledge of other countries, especially as they were hoping to increase tourism on Carathi over the forthcoming years. They had also been swayed by the fact that Ashan was in London and would keep an eye on Liyana.

And to be fair they had seen how much Liyana had wanted to go.

Of course, there had been other rules and restrictions in place. Liyana had been accompanied by a live-in royal staff member, a flat in a quiet area of London had been rented rather than allowing Liyana to share with other students or use student accommodation. And she had kept a low profile, very few people were aware of her royal status, she didn't go out partying or date and so she had stayed pretty much under the radar.

But nevertheless, she loved the relative freedom; the ability to walk around London, sightseeing, the ability to wear jeans and a top and blend in with a crowd. But now her time in London was coming to an end. There were two more weeks left, weeks where, by a stroke of fate, she was unchaperoned. Her chaperone had been called back to Carathi due to a family situation and to Liyana's surprise her parents had decided it wasn't worth sending someone to replace her for such a short time.

And so, she wanted to enjoy and appreciate every moment of the two weeks, knowing they might never come her way again. Had hoped that tonight she could put a foot onto the wild side.

But in truth she couldn't blame Ashan for his stance. He had assured their parents that he would be responsible for his sister and he wouldn't risk taking her with him. Because their people would be scandalised at their princess partying in London, even under Ashan's chaperonage. So she did get it, knew it had been a long shot, tried to keep the disappointment from her voice. 'OK. I understand.'

'Thank you, Lili, and I *am* sorry.'

She knew he was, but she also knew that he didn't get it. Couldn't completely empathise. In truth she wasn't sure she understood it herself. She'd always chafed against the strict etiquette required of a princess but this feeling was different, more than that, a *need* to not let these two weeks slip away. An urge that escalated as she left the hotel and, instead of heading back to her flat, she walked the busy streets of London, lost herself in the throng of people, spared a glance for the iconic London department stores, brightly lit to illuminate the artful displays of designer merchandise. Until an hour later she realised she'd come full circle, back to the hotel.

Just as Ashan and his group were leaving, no doubt having had a couple of cocktails in the bar. Liyana ducked out of sight, watched the mix of laughing young men and women. Women who were allowed to go for a night out. Maybe even dance on a table or two. Even as she told herself to get over herself, she couldn't swallow down a sense of envy, a desire to run across and join them.

Once they'd gone, hailing a couple of black cabs and jumping in, Liyana knew she quite simply could not go tamely home; instead, she found herself heading for the hotel, through the door and back into the lobby, only this time she didn't stop, this time she kept walking, headed towards the cocktail bar.

It might not be much. But she was going to sit in that bar and have a cocktail, do some people-watching. *Then* she would head home. For an instant she faltered as she entered the cocktail lounge, aware of the enormity of what she was doing, reminded herself that here it was perfectly acceptable to enter a bar alone and order a drink.

She glanced round to locate the best place to sit, somewhere where she was least likely to be noticed. Took in the opulence of the space, the oil paintings on the walls depicting exotic animals. The brocaded regency furniture themed in red and green, sofas and padded chairs surrounding dark wood tables. The place buzzing with people. She made her way across the plush red carpet and sat at one of the corner tables, sank into the comfort of a small sofa and studied the drinks menu, took her time deciding. After all, she didn't actually drink very often, so she might as well make it count.

Ten minutes later she took a small appreciative sip of her signature martini and then glanced around, discreetly studying the smiling, chattering congregation of people. Couples, friends, work colleagues; she was the only lone person and suddenly despite the numbers she felt a prickle of unease. Turning her head slightly, she saw a blond man gazing at her from the bar. She looked away quickly but not before he smiled and winked, before turning to his companion and saying something with a laugh.

Liyana shifted slightly so she was hopefully no longer in his line of vision as ramifications occurred to her. What if someone approached her? Worse, what if someone did recognise her? It was all very well citing the 'no publicity' rule but there were some people in London who knew her. Or what if she somehow ended up in the background of someone else's photo and ended up on social media. There might be nothing technically wrong with her sitting here with a drink on her own, but it was something she could never do at home on Carathi and she knew her parents would be horrified. She could picture her mother, shaking her head, her brown eyes full of disappointment, telling her, *'Princesses do not drink alone in public places. It is not sensible, Liyana.'* Followed by the mantra that she had heard so many times in her life. *'You need to think before you act, Liyana.'*

Liyana took another sip of her drink, prepared to abandon the whole enterprise, but as she shifted along the sofa, she saw a man enter the bar and for some reason she froze, looked and kept looking, seemingly unable not to. Blinking, she told herself to get a grip. Yet still her entire focus was on the man as he glanced round.

He was tall, looked to be about her own age, early twenties at most. His dark hair was unruly, as though he didn't have time to cut it. His lithe movements spoke of an easy power, a focused energy. He paused and scanned the room and she was so intent on watching him she failed to notice the approach of the blond man she'd spotted earlier.

Until, 'Hello, beautiful.'

Liyana quelled the urge to roll her eyes;

after all, she had been brought up learning how to defuse scenes without creating publicity, to always behave with decorum.

Whilst she was deciding what to do, the blond man sat next to her, slid along the seat and gave what he probably thought was a winning smile.

Liyana considered her options. 'I'd appreciate it if you'd leave,' she said tightly. 'I'm not interested.'

'At least let me buy you another of these cocktails and see if I can change your mind. A beautiful girl like you, sitting here on your own. It's wrong. And surely you felt something when our glances met.'

'Most likely it made her feel slightly queasy,' a voice interjected. Liyana looked up and her eyes widened as she saw the dark-haired man standing by the table. 'You heard the lady,' he said now. 'She asked you to leave, so leave.'

The blond man's colour heightened and Liyana felt panic start to ripple inside her. The very last thing she wanted here and now was a brawl; the thought of the possible headlines made her stomach clench. She had to do something.

So, 'Hello, darling,' she said and smiled up at the man. 'This is what happens when you are late. I was just about to explain I was waiting for someone.' With an effort she managed the smallest of smiles at the blond man. 'I'm sorry, but, as you can see, I'm already with someone.'

The blond man eyed the newcomer, then he shrugged. 'Fair play,' he said. 'Sorry, man.' With that he left and Liyana sent an imploring look at her saviour, who gave a small frown but then sat on the seat opposite her.

Seeing the blond man's eyes still on them, Liyana reached out and took the stranger's hand in hers and bit back a small gasp. What on earth? She'd swear sparks had arced across the table. Surely his clasp shouldn't be doing this to her, making her feel as though all she could focus on was his touch, one that sent a shiver running over her. Looking up, she saw surprise in his dark blue eyes, surprise and more than a spark of heat.

'Thank you,' she said softly.

'You're welcome. You didn't have to pretend we're together though. I would have made him leave.'

'I'd rather not have a scene. Though obviously this is now a bit problematic, especially as I don't know your name.'

'I'm Lorenzo Cavendish. And you are?'

Two things dawned on Liyana simultaneously. This man was one of Ashan's friends. And he didn't know who she was. And right now, Liyana was glad that she was under the radar, because suddenly she knew she wanted to keep it that way, didn't want to tell Lorenzo her true identity.

'I'm Elina Perera,' she said. Once again, her mother's face popped into her head and now there was an element of panic in the imagined voice. *'What are you doing, Liyana? Stop. Think.'*

Lorenzo studied his companion, wondered what the hell was going on. Yes, she was beautiful; no one could doubt that. Dark hair pulled back and upward, allowing a few tendrils to frame a classic face, high cheekbones, a delicate curve of a jaw given character by a determined chin and a straight sweep of nose. Long-lashed large brown eyes, a dark brown flecked with hints of amber. Yet his initial reaction hadn't been about beauty; his original instinct had been immediate, an innate urge to protect her. His twin sister, Daisy, would call it his Knight Errant Complex. But it hadn't been that; sure, he'd step in to prevent anyone being harassed but not usually that swiftly or on so little provocation. But he'd seen Elina's face and he'd seen a smidgeon of panic. And he'd stepped in ready to pick Blondie up by the scruff off his neck and eject him from the booth.

Instead, Elina had come up with a completely unnecessary ploy to get rid of the man. *Then* she'd taken his hand and kaboom. There wasn't any other word for it. Instant, off-the-scale, red-hot attraction. And he wasn't sure what to do about it.

The obvious answer was nothing. He was not in the market for a relationship. Had no intention of letting anything distract him from his purpose. Lorenzo was going to be a success; he was going to take his business idea and he was going to make it work. He was going to be rich and successful. He was going to show his father that he was not a failure, not a disappointment, not a joke. And, damn it, if he was rich enough, successful enough, surely his mother would finally leave. Leave a miserable marriage where she never knew if she was coming or going, bullied and humiliated some of the time, lavished with gifts the next, all in the name of love.

Something he would never understand. His mother insisted that she and Matt loved each other. They had met when they were both in their early twenties, had got married young and had twins, Lorenzo and Daisy, very soon after. Lorenzo suspected that perhaps they had got married because his mother had fallen pregnant. Lorenzo had no idea what their relationship had been like before children. But for all his life he had *known* that his father did not love him. Knew too that Matt did love Daisy, in so much as Matt 'loved' anyone. He had been kind to Daisy, supportive, willing to spend time with her, had told her he loved her. Whatever love meant—in truth it was a meaningless four-letter word that held such potential and promise and, in reality, was a yoke and a burden. A carrot and a stick.

Something Matt held out as the prize, occasionally granted if everyone pleased him enough. A prize Daisy was somehow able to win, a prize his mum sometimes won and a prize that Lorenzo never, ever achieved. Which surely meant that there was something lacking in him, something eminently unloveable. The idea was reinforced by his mother; because whilst she claimed to love him, and Matt believed she did, she never stood up for him against Matt's bullying. The way he put

Lorenzo down at any given opportunity, rejected any overture he made.

In some ways Lorenzo could understand this: his mother was a gentle, timid soul and if she did try to defend Lorenzo it did no good. Matt simply turned on them both. Lorenzo could still recall the stark stab of hurt he'd felt when Matt had crumpled up the picture he'd spent ages on for Father's Day, the sound of the derisive laugh cutting into him. The shake of Matt's head—'He just doesn't get it, does he, darling?' he'd asked Daisy as he'd accepted her drawing.

And his mum had said nothing, later hugging Lorenzo, but telling him he needed to try harder. But however hard he tried the prize was never won, so perhaps it was simply true—the fault lay with him. Within him.

The only person who he believed did love him was Daisy; he was thankful for that, though he often wondered if Daisy loved him because she had to due to some intractable rules of twinship, or because of the guilt she felt that Matt treated them so differently. Daisy was the golden child and Lorenzo was little better than dirt on the bottom of a shoe.

In the end Lorenzo had stopped trying to make sense of it all, had come to realise that the Cavendish family dynamic worked better when he was absent, that his presence exacerbated Matt's anger with his wife, made Daisy have to work harder to keep the peace, and so Lorenzo had long since given up even trying to be part of the family unit. Now his focus was on success, making it big.

But that required dedication and focus, so no way would he let a relationship distract him. He shouldn't really even be here, had very nearly declined Ashan's invitation. But then he'd recalled their friendship, unlikely but none the less true, forged at university. Lorenzo had barely had time to make friends during his three years as a student; had held down three jobs and studied. He'd met Ashan whilst delivering pizzas to him and a bunch of friends. Ashan had recognised him from campus and somehow from that unlikely beginning a genuine friendship had formed.

Ashan had been there for him, and when he'd refused monetary help instead Ashan had helped in other ways, ways that Lorenzo had truly appreciated. Because despite his royalty, his status, his popularity, all the reasons to not give Lorenzo so much as the time of day, Ashan had accepted him, actually appeared to *like* him for himself. The novelty of the idea still stunned him and so he'd turned up tonight and what he *should* do now was end this and go and find Ashan.

Yet he wanted to stay right here. With this woman. He didn't get it, but it was what he wanted. Could even justify because Ashan wasn't actually expecting him tonight; Lorenzo had told him he'd join the festivities the following day. He'd only turned up today because he'd finished a shift unexpectedly early.

She was studying his face now, her brown eyes dark and intent, almost as if she were trying to read his mind, trying to come to some decision.

'So what happens next?' she asked and glanced down.

He followed her gaze, half surprised to see their still clasped hands. Yet neither of them let go and he could almost see the fizzing connection that seemed to be wrapping around them.

'What do you want to happen next?' he asked.

'Honestly?' Her voice was low, husky, and he felt the haze of desire thicken.

'Yes.'

She took a deep breath. 'Before I answer can I ask another question?'

'Go ahead.'

She took a sip of her drink, a drink that was still nearly full. 'Do you ever have an impulse to do something completely out of character—because just for a day you want to be someone different?'

The question made him pause; he recognised its seriousness and he considered his answer. There had been plenty of times as a child when he'd imagined being someone different. Being someone who his father could love. So yes, he'd tried to be someone different; he'd tried so very hard. Tried to be perfectly behaved—his father had deemed him to be lily-livered. Tried to be naughty—that had translated into disrespectful and deserving of a 'hiding'. He'd tried to be sporty, to learn everything about his dad's favourite football team. So many things. Until he'd figured it out. His father just didn't like him. Full stop.

And there wasn't a thing he could do about it.

Lorenzo shook the thoughts away.

That had been then. That had been different; it hadn't been about a pretence for a day. He'd have been willing to change for life to win his father's approval, let alone love.

In the here and now he was focused on his

plan. Had no impulse to behave out of character. Or be anyone different. 'No,' he said bluntly. And then, 'Not until right now.' He studied her face. 'Why do you ask?'

She took a deep breath. 'Because today I want to be someone different. I want to be someone who acts on impulse, someone who has fun.' Her brown eyes met his and now a jolt ran through him. 'I know it sounds mad but I'd like to spend a few hours with you. I know I don't know you, but…maybe that's the charm of it. I don't know you; you don't know me.' Her brown eyes lit up and then she gave a sudden shake of her head. 'I'm sorry. I hadn't even thought—obviously you have plans. I know that.'

'Do you?' He looked at her, instinct telling him something was slightly off.

'I mean. You must have plans. I assume that's why you came in here? To meet someone.'

'I was due to possibly meet a group of people. But it looks like I missed them.' He met her gaze. 'So what did you have in mind?' he asked, then, aware that those words could be misconstrued, 'I mean, we could go for dinner, or stay here or…' He broke off, tried to think what might constitute having fun, tried to remember the last time he'd had fun.

Realised he couldn't. Because he was too consumed by the need to succeed. But maybe for a few hours he could seize the moment. 'Or we could figure it out as we go.'

'That sounds like a plan.'

As she spoke a waiter materialised by the table. 'A drink?' he asked.

Lorenzo nodded, glanced briefly at the menu. 'Seeing as this is where it all starts, I'll have a Kensington,' he said.

Elina waited until the waiter returned with the drink, then tipped her head to one side. 'You chose it because of its name? What if you don't like it?'

'That's a risk I'll take, but for tonight I thought it would be nice to go with the flow and see where it takes me. That's the idea, isn't it?'

She smiled, a smile so wide he found himself smiling back, a heady sense of freedom touching him. 'Yes, it is. For a few hours let's not think about our real lives.'

He frowned. 'Is your real life so bad?' he asked.

For a moment she looked slightly stricken. 'No.' She shook her head. 'It isn't. But my family… It's difficult sometimes. I mean, I love them very much but they have old-fashioned ideas.'

Lorenzo hesitated. 'Even though you live here?'

There was a slight hesitation, as if she was weighing her words. 'Even so.'

'What do they do?'

'They run a family company,' Elina said. 'My father is the CEO and my mother helps. He always says he couldn't do it without her, but nonetheless it is his company and, if push comes to shove, if they disagree on a strategy, he has the final say.' She shrugged. 'And I understand that. It is his family company. But they have rules and expectations for me that stem from our culture. And I understand that too. But just for tonight I suppose I'd like to escape them. Break a few rules. That's why I ended up in here drinking a cocktail on my own. It was a minor act of rebellion. My plan was to drink my drink, do a little people-watching and head home. But then…then I met you and now…' She shrugged. 'I'm enjoying your company and I'd like to have a few more hours where I forget the rules. If that's what you want too.'

Lorenzo thought for a moment. Elina came

from a sheltered background and a culture with its own expectations. 'I don't want you to get into trouble or do anything that you regret,' he said finally. Seeing the quickly veiled look of hurt on her face, he realised she thought he was rejecting her. 'I do want to spend the next few hours with you. I really do. The last few years of my life I've been so focused on work, on fulfilling my ambition, that I haven't done anything spontaneous in as long as I can remember. I would love to put that aside for a few hours. But not if it causes a problem for you.'

'It won't.' Her voice held conviction. 'It can't. A few hours…that's all it would be. Then of course I will go back to my life. I do understand the importance of my family culture and traditions. I want a taste of something else, a memory to look back on. With *you*…' She paused, flicked a glance to the bar where the blond man still sat. 'It is important for me that you know I would not suggest this to just anyone, this is not what I was looking for when I came in here.'

'And I want you to know that you can trust me.'

She smiled at him, a smile that lit her brown

eyes, flecked them with amber. ‘I do trust you,’ she said.

‘Then let’s go.’ He rose to his feet and held out his hand and as she placed hers in his, he felt it again. Kaboom.

CHAPTER ONE

Seven years later, Royal Palace, Carathi

LIYANA STARED AT her reflection, willed her expression to retain the serene neutrality she had practised until it was perfect. Tugged and pinned another errant strand of hair. Told herself she was being utterly ridiculous—after everything that had happened over the past seven years, the seismic amount of water that had torrented under the bridge, it was ridiculous to be feeling nervous at the idea of seeing Lorenzo Cavendish again.

Yes, their parting had been less than amicable but they had both moved on in the intervening years.

For a moment she allowed herself to recall that night, the sheer magical element to it. They'd left the hotel and wandered the streets of London, hand in hand, talking about anything and everything. Hopped on a Tube and ended up at an indoor food market, where they'd sampled different street foods, dumplings and sushi, followed by late-night ice-cream cones, eaten as they'd walked under the now moonlit sky. For an instant she could almost taste the cold, smooth mint taste, the tang of the dark chocolate chips, the laughter when she'd ended up with an ice-cream 'moustache', the electric sensation when he'd run a finger around her mouth to remove it.

They'd come to a halt under the stars, she'd looked up at him and she wasn't sure who had moved towards who but, somehow, she'd been in his arms and his lips had covered hers and… As clichéd as it was, it had felt as though there were fireworks. The sheer mind-blowing wonder of it had made her dizzy, had filled her with yearning and joy, need and delight.

They'd eventually broken apart, staring at each other in shock. Liyana had known what she should do. She should have walked away but she hadn't been able to—the sense of connection, the desire, the sheer exultation coursing her veins had made that impossible. Perhaps too she should have told him then who she was, but how could she have done? The heady knowledge that Lorenzo had no idea of her identity, was attracted to her as a person, not a princess, combined with the suspicion that he would walk away if he knew the truth had stopped the words.

Instead, she'd stepped back into his embrace and after that there had been no real coherent thought, they'd gone back to her flat and once there…

Back in the present Liyana raised hands to her flushed cheeks, pushed away the memories of passion, laughter, tenderness and marvel, their bodies so attuned, the hours so full of joy.

And then the morning where it had all gone so wrong. When all the consequences she should have foreseen, should have considered, had come crashing in.

Enough. It was over. Done with. History. No longer important, the raw emotions diluted by the events of the past seven years. It was surely foolish that the memory of that single night was so vivid, so powerful, given all that had happened since.

Two years after Lorenzo, she'd met Gregor Mertens: incredibly good-looking, charming and famous in his own right. A Formula One champion driver with a legion of fans, wealthy in his own right, Gregor had swept her off her feet. Dazzled her, infatuated her, offered her so much she had thought impossible: love and freedom from all the restrictions imposed by her royalty. And so when he'd made a public proposal, she'd agreed, dizzy with the novelty, the belief he'd loved her for herself.

She'd known her parents had reservations, known they were hurt to discover the relationship through a breaking story. But, in the end, they had had little choice in the matter. The press had jumped on the story of Gregor's whirlwind romance and there had been no going back. So, they had made the best of it. After all, Gregor's wealth and fame had brought publicity to the island and they had hoped that perhaps it would help increase tourism, that Gregor and Liyana could act as ambassadors.

The wedding had graced the pages of every magazine, every news publication in the world. And for a while Liyana had been happy…or she'd told herself she was. When had it dawned on her that the man she'd married was not the man she'd believed him to be? She had believed he loved her for herself; turned out he'd wanted to add a princess to his trophies. She'd believed he'd be faithful; turned out he hadn't believed in fidelity. He'd believed his fame and looks made him 'different' from other men, that he could play by different rules because, after all, his job had meant his life was on the line so he had to live it.

Liyana felt the thump of guilt, of grief, of sadness, the emotions a dark vortex that threatened to suck her in if she let it. Because Gregor hadn't lived; three years after their wedding he'd died in a tragic crash, not on the racetrack but in his own sports car, a swerve round a bend, on a storm-swept night, in torrential rain and wind, he'd lost control and plummeted over a cliff.

The memory triggered the familiar complexity of emotion. The grief at the tragic loss of a man in his prime, a man who had loved and lived life to the full, a man who she had once at least believed she'd loved. But alongside that grief was the insidious, pervading knowledge that his death had freed her from the shackles of a marriage she had been trapped in. Trapped by the royal duty she had to her country to avoid the taint and scandal of divorce. Trapped too perhaps by her own need to make the impossible work, a belief that if she tried hard enough, she could somehow resurrect the dream.

Any which way Gregor's death had freed her to come home and live her life. The knowledge a constant burr of guilt: how could she possibly find any positive in tragedy, the loss of a life? So, she did all she could, what she at least owed his memory. To keep the myth alive. That she had loved him, that their marriage had been idyllic, that she was a grieving widow in every sense of the word.

As for love, sometimes Liyana wondered if she had ever truly loved Gregor or if she'd been in love with the idea of being in love. Of living her own life for herself, with a man who she had believed loved her for herself rather than a marriage of duty. Escaping her identity, just as she had that night with Lorenzo.

So here she was full circle again. Back to thoughts of Lorenzo.

Who she was going to see all too soon.

Nerves began to beat, and Liyana had the lowering feeling that her pulse rate had ratcheted. She needed to get a grip. The important thing here was that in a few months Ashan was getting married. To a neighbouring princess. Lorenzo was the best man. Liyana was the wedding planner in chief. Tonight was a 'family and close friend' gathering to celebrate. So, they would have to meet. She would make sure it was civil, discreet and brief. With any luck, once she actually saw him, she would gain some much-needed perspective, be able to relegate that night to its rightful place. One night. A blip. In the scheme of things an unimportant mistake best forgotten. Liyana took one last glance at her reflection and turned to leave.

Lorenzo took a deep breath, inhaled the sun-warmed air laced with subtle floral tones of hibiscus and took in the architectural sprawl of the Carathian palace. The edifice was massive and magnificent, with Tudor-style towers and battlements, ornate stained-glass windows and detailed wooden carvings. The whole set in enormous grounds that boasted gardens that Ashan had told him were the pride of the area, rivalling the famed botanic gardens of neighbouring Sri Lanka.

Despite his long friendship with Ashan, Lorenzo had never visited Carathi, and he fully intended to use his time here to explore. He'd taken a month's break from work, though he would of course stay in touch and oversee from afar, wouldn't be able to completely cut himself off from the company that had made him millions, the company that he had built from scratch into a global enterprise. Customers all over the world relied on Take It Away, his brainchild, the result of taking an idea and nourishing and tending and growing it into a global entity.

Lorenzo was proud of Take It Away, a company that prided itself on delivering food from restaurant door to customer fresh and edible. Proud of how he'd achieved it, through sheer grit and hard work, holding down multiple jobs, living in his car, saving his capital and negotiating a start-up loan. Yet that pride had been tarnished by recent events. Events seemed like way too bland a word for the tumult, the shock, the sheer cold burn of anger that ran through him as he tried to process the knowledge that the man he'd believed to be his father, the father he'd burned and striven to prove wrong, was not in fact his father.

A few months ago, he and Daisy had discovered that their mother had lied, had told Matt Cavendish that she was pregnant with his children when in fact their 'real' father had been an Italian vintner, Roberto Rossi. A married man who had walked away the moment he'd discovered Karen was pregnant, had stayed away even once informed of Lorenzo and Daisy's birth. A man who had died when Lorenzo was still a child, but Roberto's father was still alive and so was his other daughter.

So now Lorenzo and Daisy had a grandfather and a half-sister.

Lorenzo had visited the Tuscan vineyard that had been 'in the family' for generations. Had met Vittorio Rossi and Amara Rossi. But he hadn't been back, despite an open and clearly sincere invitation, despite their new family's seemingly genuine wish to welcome Lorenzo and Daisy in.

Because Lorenzo wasn't sure he wanted an entrée to the Rossi family The thought of being a family scared him, especially a family that worked. The bond between his half-sister and their grandfather was clear to see, forged over years. How could he intrude on that? How could he become part of that? How would he know what to do? Wasn't it better, easier, to just stay aloof?

Lorenzo told himself this was not the time to dwell on the revelations that had upturned his life. This was about his friend, about Ashan. He was here in his role of best man. He had a month on this beautiful island to think. And part of what he wanted to think about was the future he wanted his upended life to take. The idea that, although Take It Away would always be a part of his business life, it was time to do something new, something more worthy. Not motivated by wanting to prove something but by wanting to do something good. But that was for later.

Right now, he had other things to worry about, could feel a nervous tension, a ridiculous tremor of nerves, run through his gut. Because like it or not Princess Liyana would undoubtedly be in attendance.

Not that it mattered. What had happened between them was lost in the past, something that had once been important. Yes, at the time he'd been furious at her deception, but now, seven years later, he knew it was just one night between two people whose lives had moved on. Liyana had found love and happiness and then experienced tragedy. Their night together would have faded to complete insignificance; they could meet now as the strangers everyone believed them to be,

So there was no need for any jitter of nerves. Entering through open wrought-iron gates adorned with royal insignia, he walked down the gravelled pathway flanked by statues and lush potted trees towards the entrance, showed the security detail his official invitation and was ushered inside. He followed a staff member down a long marble-floored corridor, the wood-panelled walls lined with portraits of past kings and queens.

As they walked another usher approached them and had a quick word before heading off.

'Please wait here for a moment, Mr Cavendish.' Lorenzo forced himself not to flinch, yet somehow every time his surname was used it was a reminder that if life had been different, he would be Lorenzo Rossi. Because it was Rossi blood that ran through his veins. Perhaps the knowledge should make him happy, but Roberto Rossi hadn't given him a chance at all. Had rejected him without ever meeting him.

Was that better or worse than Matt's rejection? Lorenzo shook the thoughts away; sometimes he wished he and Daisy had never found the truth. A truth they didn't know what to do with; they hadn't even told Karen that they knew it. Lorenzo was still in shock, still trying to process how his mother could have done it, lived a lie for so long.

A minute later and Ashan strode towards him, a smile on his face. 'Lorenzo. You're here. Great to see you.'

'You too,' Lorenzo said, shook hands and then allowed his friend to catch him in a bear hug.

'Come this way. Before we join the guests,

I wanted you to meet my fiancée more privately.'

'Sure.'

'There's something we'd like to say to you.'

Lorenzo glanced at his friend. 'Everything OK?'

'Never better. I…we just have a favour to ask.'

Ashan pushed a door open and stepped back to allow Lorenzo in first. Lorenzo stepped over the doorstep and froze.

Sitting around a table were two women, both of whom rose to their feet. Two women but Lorenzo had eyes for only one. It really was Liyana. His eyes seemed to drink her in, his brain seeing the similarities and the differences. The glorious cascade of hair he recalled was scraped back tightly into a bun, the brown eyes held wariness and a definite hint of what? Panic?

The same as he felt.

Desire?

The same as he felt.

Enough. He'd told himself that this wouldn't be a problem and he wouldn't let it be. There was no reason for this fizz of desire, this electrifying jolt as if the air had charged. It must simply be the unexpectedness that had sucker-punched him.

'I'd like you to meet my fiancée.' Ashan's voice, with its hint of puzzlement, broke through the spell and Lorenzo pulled himself together, turned away from Liyana and smiled at the other woman, registered brown eyes, a heart-shaped face and curly hair that fell to her shoulders. 'This is Kaveesha.'

He could hear the pride in Ashan's voice and he held his hand out. 'I am very pleased to meet you,' he said.

'And this is my sister, Liyana,' Ashan continued and Lorenzo turned back. 'Nangi, this is Lorenzo. I can't believe the two of you have never met.'

Neither could he. Lorenzo kept his lips upturned, hoped his smile looked natural, polite. Hoped no one could hear the accelerated thud of his heart, see the clench of his jaw.

'It's good to meet you,' he said, braced himself and held his hand out, knew he had no choice but knew it was a mistake nonetheless.

Saw her almost imperceptible hesitation and then she put her hand in his.

And kaboom. Again.

Lorenzo could only hope his intake of breath hadn't been heard, knew there was way too much hoping going on. Her eyes widened in shock and he saw somewhere in the brown depths an amber spark of sheer desire. Succeeded by a flash of panic and another of anger and then it was gone. Her face took on a neutrality, her voice low and polite, her smile the exact right wattage level.

'And you,' she said and he would almost have been taken in except he realised they were still holding hands, just as they had years before, as if their instinct was to hold on, not let go. Because whatever her voice was saying, however in control she looked, he was damn sure she could feel the current running between them, causing a heat to burn in his gut, bringing back memories that he knew needed to be pushed down and forgotten. They were from a past that was over. That Liyana and Lorenzo did not exist any more.

Ashan and Kaveesha exchanged glances and then Ashan gestured to the table. 'Now introductions are over, Kaveesha and I were hoping to have a chat with both of you.'

Minutes later they were all seated.

'We have a favour to ask,' Ashan said. 'And we realised you two are the only people we can really trust to do it.'

'We will of course understand if you don't

agree, but we hope you will consider it,' Kaveesha added. 'It is truly important to us.'

Lorenzo was getting a bad feeling about this, a sense of foreboding spiralling in the pit of his stomach. One he sensed Liyana shared; despite her calm expression he could see the tension in her body, in the slight set of her jaw. For a moment his gaze threatened to focus on the curve of her jaw line, the combination of character and delicacy in the clean line. He forced his gaze not to move to her lips as more memories threatened. He had to get a grip. She was a widow. Her husband, the man she had adored according to every newspaper article he hadn't been able to avoid seeing over the years, was dead, had died a tragic death two years before.

This spark, volt thing was a figment of his imagination.

Only somehow, he knew it wasn't.

Kaveesha took a deep breath. 'As you both know, in three months' time Ashan and I are due to be married. It will be a massive event, a wedding for the people, a wedding that brings good publicity to the island and helps boost the economy and support for the monarchy and we know how important that is. But…'

'We'd like our wedding to be more than

that.' Ashan's smile as he looked at his fiancée was full of love and filled Lorenzo with a sudden shaft of... Not envy but perhaps surprise. His understanding had been that this marriage was arranged, one of duty. 'Of course, in three months we will have the public ceremony, smile for the cameras, do everything that is expected of us. Do our duty.'

Next to him he felt Liyana flinch slightly.

'But we would also like a private ceremony. Something that is just for us, to mark our love for each other, mark our commitment.'

'You want an extra wedding,' Liyana said.

Ashan nodded. 'A private ceremony; there is no way we can organise it ourselves, not without some public attention. But we thought that maybe you both could. Together?'

Together. Him and Liyana. Bad, bad idea. But there were other reasons it was a bad idea.

Lorenzo tried for a smile. 'I am truly flattered at your trust but I know nothing about weddings.' And even less about love.

'No, but Liyana does. She is already part of planning the public wedding, but she is more in the public domain. You aren't. So we thought somehow, between you, you may be able to pull it off.' Kaveesha looked at him imploringly as Ashan looked at Liyana.

'It's important, Lili,' he said. 'It doesn't have to be fancy or expensive or anything—just… private. For us.'

Liyana bit her lip and Lorenzo knew that she had no choice. Any more than he did. He was Ashan's best man. She was Ashan's sister.

'I'll do it,' she said softly now. 'Of course I will. But there is no need for Lorenzo to get involved.'

'Yes, there is,' Ashan said firmly. 'For a start, you are doing enough and I won't burden you with sole responsibility for this.'

Kaveesha reached out and covered Liyana's hand. 'I know it is a lot to ask and perhaps unfair but…'

Liyana pulled her hand away, gently but decisively. 'It is perfectly fair and I am perfectly capable.'

'We know that,' Ashan said. 'But I'd like Lorenzo to be involved. It makes sense. He can fly under the radar more, make arrangements without undue publicity or alerting the press. What do you think?'

'Of course I'm in.' What else could he say? 'When were you hoping to have the ceremony?'

'I know it's a lot to ask but we were hoping

in the next couple of weeks, if at all possible,' Kaveesha said.

'That way there is less chance of attracting undue notice.' He saw Liyana glance at her brother as he spoke, a slight crease to her forehead. Ashan rose to his feet. 'Now I think we'd better mingle. We're going to spread the word that you are part of team wedding and that I've asked Liyana to show you around the island. That will give the two of you a chance to liaise without suspicion.'

Liaise. He and Liyana were going to liaise. This was not what he'd had in mind at all. But what could he say? Except, 'That sounds great.'

'We thought you may want to have a chat and of course get started as soon as possible, so I've booked you a private table at the Chandraya Bar tonight.' Kaveesha's voice was brisk now the situation was settled.

Better and better. The only comfort was that a quick glance showed Liyana looked as horrified as he did, though within seconds the expression was wiped from her face and she smiled. 'Perfect,' she said.

CHAPTER TWO

PERFECT SHMERFECT. AFTER a couple of hours of social mingling, Liyana once again stood in front of her mirror glaring at her reflection. Only this time behind her on the bed was a scattered selection of discarded clothes options. She'd wanted to change from the formal dress expected for a royal social gathering into something more casual. Casual but professional. Something professional, muted, something that gave out the right signals. Because right now her hormones had identified, or perhaps she should say reidentified, Lorenzo as being ridiculously, scorchingly desirable. They wanted him and they were sending out signals fast and furious. The wrong signals.

Well, Liyana had news for her hormones. No can do. She was going to have a drink with Lorenzo and she was going to close this down. She was not spending days with him; not days, not hours. If Ashan knew the truth he wouldn't have asked her. But she couldn't, wouldn't, tell the truth. The idea of telling Ashan that she had slept with his best friend, explaining the deception, felt…wrong, like a betrayal of Lorenzo. He had been truly horrified when he'd discovered her identity, realised he'd slept with his friend's sister, and Liyana still felt a pang of guilt at her deception.

So, she would not tell the secret that had been kept for so many years; there was no need for Ashan to know. Equally though she could not spend more time with Lorenzo. It was too awkward. Not only because of their shared past but because she was embarrassingly still attracted to him. Which made life complicated.

Liyana didn't want complications, didn't like or understand how a mere half an hour with Lorenzo had unsettled her. More than unsettled her—when he'd walked into the room her whole body had reacted, her tummy had lurched, her pulse rate had ratcheted and when her hand had clasped his, her head had spun, the touch electrifying. Triggering memories that should have surely muted long ago but instead had played out in vivid colour.

Liyana scowled at her reflection; she did not need this right now, when she had a massive decision hanging over her head. A decision she was determined to make logically, calmly. A decision that would affect the rest of her life and to make it she needed a clear head. After Gregor's death and her return to Carathi, Liyana had vowed she would never again be ruled by impulse or attraction. Love and freedom had turned out to be a mirage and a trap so now she would focus on doing her duty, doing good for her country. And she had, had worked hard and tirelessly with results she was proud of. Now a neighbouring kingdom had expressed an interest in arranging a marriage between their prince and Liyana. A marriage that would bring trade benefits and cement a solid alliance. She needed to consider the option carefully; she did not need to feel unsettled or distracted.

So, she was going to make it clear to Lorenzo that this idea of Ashan and Kaveesha's was a non-starter. The good thing was she was sure he would agree, probably was going to suggest the same thing. *This* time, they would have *one* cocktail and part ways.

In which case it didn't matter what she wore. *No.* She shook her head. It always mattered. Growing up, she'd always had to look royal, demure, perfectly turned out. Life with Gregor had turned out to be much the same, in the sense he'd expected her to always look perfect. Worthy of being his wife. He'd wanted other men to envy him, wanted to display his royal trophy. Liyana had spent their three years of marriage dressing as he'd wished her to dress, spent hours making sure she was 'up to scratch', as he'd put it. Not that he'd even appreciated it—he'd expected it, taken delight in keeping her on tenterhooks, compared her to other women, models, superstars. To him, they had been the competition and he had been the prize.

Now she was back to being a princess, and she dressed to be unnoticed, wanted to be taken seriously, was happy to work in the background. Though all that would change if she agreed to marry Prince Luis. A decision that hung over her head like the sword of Damocles, the pros and cons jostling in her brain; she was aware one must take precedence soon. But first she had to deal with the Lorenzo issue.

One last glance at her reflection, a nod of approval at the sober grey tunic, threaded with just a hint of blue over matching grey trousers, and she once again turned for the door.

Twenty minutes later she exited the car with

a smile and a wave to her driver, a staff member who had known her since childhood, and entered the bar, tucked into a coconut grove, nestled on the edge of a beach. Followed the manager through the busy ground floor where customers surrounded the bar, where the staff worked in a whir producing cocktails that drew customers from all over the country. Then through to the private area requested by Ashan, a small additional shanty, built with local materials, the roof tiles propped up by coconut-tree pillars. The tables made from recycled beach driftwood, handmade tabletops, with the bar's motif baked in.

Lorenzo stood to greet her and she forced her steps to remain even, hoped that her face remained neutral, polite.

Why did he have to look so gorgeous? Because there was no other word to describe him. Dressed simply in a black T-shirt and jeans, he had her whole body on high alert. Exactly how she had felt seven years ago; how was it possible for the pull to still be so strong? She couldn't help it, knew her gaze was lingering a fraction too long on the swell of his shoulders, the bulk of his chest, and now when she met his gaze, and saw the way he was looking at her, a shiver ran over her skin. Because there was a heat in his arresting blue eyes, and the knowledge that he was as affected as her sent a visceral sense of satisfaction through her.

She had to get a grip. Before anyone noticed anything. Forcing herself to step forward, she managed a smile. 'It's good to see you, Lorenzo. Hopefully we can have a productive meeting.'

Liyana sat down, busied herself with studying the cocktail menu. Why, oh, why did Ashan have to have chosen a cocktail bar as a venue? The whole thing too evocative of memories she was trying to suppress. She stared down at the menu and every title seemed to hold a hidden meaning. Giving up, she smiled at the waiter. 'What would you recommend?' she asked.

'The owner has just come up with a new recipe. Rum, absinthe and coconut with a sour kick.'

'That sounds good.'

'I'll have the same,' Lorenzo said.

'Two Starlight Expresses coming up.' With that the waiter was gone, leaving them alone.

Starlight Express. What were the chances of that? As their gazes met, she saw a small rueful smile tug his lips and she felt her tummy clench in a sudden twist of desire as she focused on those lips, recalled that first magical kiss under the stars.

Once the drinks were in front of them, and she had thanked the waiter, Liyana took a deep breath, hoping she at least looked calm, collected and professional. Reminded herself she dealt with people all day every day nowadays in her role as Royal Advisor.

'First,' she said, 'I wanted to say I am sorry about all of this. I had no idea this was what Ashan intended.'

'I think it's safe to say he blindsided us both.'

'Yes. So, whilst clearly it was impossible to refuse his request earlier, there is absolutely no need for us to actually do what he suggested.'

Lorenzo raised his eyebrows. 'So you want to renege on an agreement, back out? *Lie?*'

Just as she had all those years ago; the implication was clear and Liyana narrowed her eyes. 'No. That is not what I meant. I have every intention of doing what I agreed to, but there is no need for you to be involved.'

'But I agreed to be involved.'

His tone was eminently reasonable and Liyana, realising this wasn't going to be as straightforward as she'd hoped, managed a smile. Which was no mean feat whilst gritting her teeth. 'I'm not explaining this very well. Of course I will keep you in the loop, give you a chance to give your opinion and if you can help in any way I will ask. You'll still be part of it. Agreed?'

There was a pause and then he shook his head. 'No,' he said. 'I appreciate this is awkward but no can do.'

'No can do?' she echoed. 'Why not?'

'Because I've done some thinking. What happened seven years ago… I won't let it stop me from being a good friend to Ashan now. He has asked for my help and I want to give it. Properly.'

Liyana heard the steel edge to the polite tone and it surprised her. She'd expected him to capitulate instantly.

'And that is understandable. Commendable,' she added. 'But there is really no need for you to help. I know the country, I know the right places, I know—'

'And the country knows you,' he countered. 'You heard what Ashan said—if you do the logistics someone will figure out what is going on.'

'And if Ashan's best man does it no one will notice? This plan is half baked at best. I will be discreet, come up with a cover story.'

'No need. I already have. I can say I am checking out venues for myself.'

An unidentifiable emotion assailed her. Was Lorenzo in a relationship? In which case this whole attraction thing was in her head.

'So you're in a relationship?' Even if he was, 'Engaged? Planning a wedding on Carathi?' Liyana made little attempt to hide the sarcasm in her tone.

'No. On all fronts.' The denial immediate and horror tinged. 'I would say that I need to check out the venues because I am thinking about offering a holiday for two on Carathi as a raffle prize for a charity gala I am hosting in six months. Whilst I'm here I want to make sure it is a viable prize, as it may be a romantic holiday or a honeymoon, I'll need to find out some relevant details. That's the premise.' He leant back and smiled at her, a smile that didn't reach his eyes. 'What do you think?'

'Not bad.'

'It even has the benefit of truth. I *will* donate a holiday for two.' His smile widened. 'It's all completely understandable and extra commendable. It is also less risky than your idea, which maximises the chances of it working. This is better for Ashan, and it's the least I can do as his friend. This is important to him and it would be foolish to let something that happened so long ago stop me…' he paused '…stop *us* from giving them what they have asked for.'

'There is no us.' The words were out before she could stop them and her brain engaged in instant disaster management. She raised her hand. 'I mean, you're right.' There was a certain logic to his words and she couldn't help but admire his sense of friendship. 'What happened then has no bearing on now.' Except for the unassailable fact that against all odds the attraction had survived, and the events of that night so long ago appeared to be etched on her memory.

'Exactly. So all we have to do is put it behind us and any awkwardness will go away. We can start again.' There was a silence as they both considered the words and Liyana wondered what it would be like to start again by going on a real date, knowing each other's identities. Like two normal people who were attracted to each other.

But that wasn't what he meant, it had just been an unfortunate choice of words and in acknowledgement he gave a sudden smile, full of rue, but this was a real smile. One that transformed his usually serious expression, relaxed the sense of drive and purpose that emanated from him, crinkled his dark blue eyes. 'We can start again as two people who are going to work together on a project without letting the past intrude.'

Liyana nodded, knew that perhaps she should simply agree, but there was a part of her that felt a sudden spark of anger. This sounded to her like an attempt to brush the whole thing away, bury it. A small voice pointed out that there was nothing wrong with the strategy, that in fact it was a good one. Another part of her wondered if he really could brush it aside that easily, tidy it up and erase the awkwardness.

'That's a good idea,' she said. 'But how exactly are we going to do that? How are we going to put the past behind us?' And what about the very present attraction? she couldn't help wondering.

There was a silence and then there was that smile again. 'I was really hoping you wouldn't ask that.' She heard the teasing lilt in his voice and Liyana couldn't help it, she laughed and he laughed too, and the sound warmed her, because she sensed that this was a man who didn't laugh often or easily.

'Maybe we need to talk about it. Clear the air,' he suggested.

'Talk about it?' Technicolour memories flooded her brain. Talk about what exactly? The sheer magic of that evening, the way he had made her feel—as if she was an interesting, attractive woman in her own right. The way they'd talked, laughed. Or did he want to talk about the night itself? The glorious heady passion, the way they had explored each other's bodies giving and receiving such dizzying pleasure. Laughter and intensity, gentleness and strength.

As their gazes met, she realised that he was walking the same steps down the same memory path and she couldn't help herself, she did allow herself to look at the strong features played on and illuminated by the dance of the candlelight, the square jaw, the jut of his nose, the deep dark mesmerising blue of his eyes. The businesslike haircut that couldn't quite hide an unruly tendency to curl, and she recalled that his hair had been longer seven years ago.

And somehow now without her even meaning it to her hand was inching towards his. The urge to touch his skin almost overwhelming. Perhaps she should. Perhaps if she did, she would realise this was all in her overheated imagination. Or the table would catch fire.

Now the moment tautened, the silence growing as she tried to work out what to do, desire rippling through her, made worse by the sheer vividness of her memories.

This had to stop.

Because it had nowhere to go. She was a widowed princess considering a marriage of convenience, a political alliance. If the press so much as caught a hint of this attraction it would be game over, marriage to Prince Luis would become a non-starter. But it was more than that. Liyana had determined never to let attraction govern her again. More than a determination, it was a *promise* she had made to herself. A lesson she had learnt the hard way; her track record abysmal. One disastrous one-night stand. One thoroughly disastrous marriage that had culminated in tragedy. There was no way she would break that vow to herself. So, in essence this attraction was impossible and an impossible attraction was nothing to fear and the knowledge made her relax a little.

She met his gaze, kept her posture relaxed but straight-backed, presenting professional princess at its best. This was under her control.

'Right. Let's get the air cleared, then we can start planning the ceremony.' She sipped her drink, tried to marshal her thoughts, her mind going back to that morning seven years before.

Waking up, feeling sleepy and sated and ridiculously happy though, at first, she couldn't recall why, the vestiges of sleep still cocooning her. Just as Lorenzo's arms had held her all night. Until finally her brain clicked into gear. Where was Lorenzo? Had he left? If he had was that good or bad? If he hadn't should she tell him who she really was? And another ridiculous thought—could she somehow keep the pretence going longer? Could they spend another day together? Could she be Elina for one more day?

Her mind raced; she had brought him back to her flat but she knew there was nothing obvious lying around. So if Lorenzo was still here then maybe she could get away with it. But somehow, as she thought about it, she knew she couldn't do that, couldn't prolong the deception—that would be wrong. But the risk of confessing the truth was too great. Wasn't it?

Back in the present, remembered guilt and hurt panged at her and she blinked. 'If it's OK, I'll start,' she said.

Lorenzo sipped his drink and studied Liyana's face, wondering why one night seven years ago still held such significance. But it did and as he looked at her now, it was as though he could see their younger selves. He was back in her flat, could feel the sock to his gut when he'd discovered who she was.

He was standing in her kitchen—Elina's kitchen, as he'd believed then. He was going to make her breakfast in bed, opened a cupboard in search of coffee and tucked into the side there was a photograph. Of a smiling Elina and a smiling Ashan, arms round each other.

He heard a sound from the door, looked up and saw Elina, standing there, looking stricken. And in the throes of hurt he jumped to the wrong conclusion.

'So this was fake all along. You are no longer with Ashan so you waited and decided one of his friends would do.'

Her face paled and he saw hurt that was quickly superseded by a flash of anger.

But he didn't care. 'Did you know who I was?' he demanded.

'Yes.' Her voice small but clear. 'But I have never been Ashan's girlfriend. I'm his sister.'

The words were another slug to the gut as his brain tried to process them and he realised the enormity of what he'd done. He knew how protective Ashan was of his younger sister, knew that his friend would be horrified by what he would see as a betrayal. And damn it, it felt like a betrayal. His voice held every nuance of his horror when he asked, 'How could you do that? I would never ever have slept with you if I'd known who you were.'

In the here and now Lorenzo reminded himself that it was in the past, the past they were putting behind them. 'Go ahead,' he said.

'First, I want to say sorry. I should never have lied to you.'

'Why did you?' At the time he hadn't even thought to ask; he'd been so shocked, so angry, so hurt, so betrayed and so conscious of how Ashan would react. He'd looked at Liyana.

'Ashan will never forgive me.'

'I won't tell Ashan.'

'Well, I won't lie to him.'

Elina stepped forward, her brown eyes full of panic. 'You can't tell him. You don't understand what that would do.'

'Maybe you should have thought about that before you lied to me.'

'Yes, I should. But...' She reached out and then dropped her hand as he stepped away, quickly concealed hurt flashing across her eyes. 'It won't gain anything to tell him. It

would have all sorts of ramifications. Our island has old-fashioned values—if anyone finds out it will bring scandal to the royal family. It will be bad for Ashan as well as for me. Nothing would be gained. If neither you nor I tell anyone then that protects Ashan. It also protects your friendship with him.'

There was a silence as he tried to process everything, aware of a sense of hurt, and anger with himself for his own folly. He should have known not to get involved, known to stick to his chosen path. 'I'll think about it,' he said. And then without even another glance at her he'd left, the door slamming shut behind him.

And he had thought about it and, in the end, he had decided not to tell Ashan, had seen that Liyana had been right. It would not have benefited anyone and so, despite his guilt, he had kept that night a secret, had tried to banish it from his mind. But in the here and now the scene was still vivid in his mind and he did want to know why Liyana had done what she'd done.

She took a deep breath and, despite the fact it was from years ago, somehow this felt important, their gazes locked and riveted. As if somehow the past and the present were colliding, the ghosts of their former selves present here. All combining and, his hand stretched out across the table to oh-so near to hers, so near they were nearly touching. And he could feel a frisson, a connection fizzing as she spoke.

'I lied because it felt so glorious for someone, for *you*, to like me. To find me attractive. The real me, not a princess. You weren't influenced by my royalty. You thought you were speaking to a student. And in that moment I wanted to be a student, not a princess.' She paused, looked at him as if she was willing him to understand. 'My whole life I had to play by the rules of my country. A princess's behaviour has to be above reproach at all times. A princess doesn't date unless it is a date with an approved man, a potential marriage partner. Even then the date would be chaperoned. My family, my people, would have been scandalised that I was in a public bar drinking on my own. And that evening I just wanted a taste of freedom, to see what it felt like to be with someone who liked me for me.'

'The blond man didn't know you were a princess. He liked you.'

'The blond man was a creep,' she said tartly.

'But you *knew* I was Ashan's friend,' he

said. 'Is that why you did it? Because I was safer than the blond man?'

'No!' He could hear the sincerity in the denial. 'I did it because I liked *you.* Because there was an instant zing from the minute you walked into the bar, before I knew who you were.' Now her hand rested briefly on his and she broke off as they both stared down, felt the exact same zing she'd described. Only this time they both knew exactly who the other person was.

'Knowing you were Ashan's friend gave me a sense of safety but I don't think it made any real difference. If I'm honest I wasn't really thinking straight. I had been intending to have one drink, my own little act of rebellion before heading home. Then you arrived and I started the whole pretence on an impulse and then it was so wonderful to be liked for myself. I never imagined that we would end up…how we did. I thought we'd maybe have another drink somewhere and then part ways, with you going off to Ashan's birthday celebrations. At most I thought we may share a kiss. I wanted to extend the feeling of being liked for me, a mutual attraction untainted by who I was. And then as the evening progressed, I just wanted… You. But now, looking back, I can see how selfish that was. I didn't give your friendship with Ashan a thought. It was…'

'Magic,' he said softly. 'As though there were only us, in a magical bubble of time.'

'Time with no consequences. Only of course there were. The next morning, I woke up and I didn't know what to do. Because I did realise *then* that if you worked out who I was I could be in big trouble. With everyone. If Ashan found out, if you went public…the scandal would have been unthinkable. And then the decision was taken out of my hands.'

'Because I found the photograph.'

'Yes, and you were so horrified; and that felt like…' She took a breath. 'I guess it felt like a rejection, and I know you had every right to feel how you felt but it just really burst the bubble.'

Lorenzo could hear remembered hurt in her voice, recalled the horror and rejection she would have seen in his eyes and in his words.

'The way you looked at me, it made everything feel tainted. Everything we'd done, everything we'd shared. I was confused and angry and I also knew I had done something wrong. I shouldn't have lied to you. But if I'd told you who I was from the start…you would never have agreed to spend time with me. It was selfish.'

Now he placed his hand over hers, heard her small intake of breath. 'No, Liyana. It wasn't. You thought we could have a few hours together.' Those had been her words. 'When you said that, when I agreed, I never thought we would end up spending the night together either. And I am sorry too. Sorry I made you feel like that.' And he was. 'I was so shocked and, yes, I was worried about Ashan.'

He hesitated, decided she deserved the truth. 'But it was more than that. I felt such a fool as well.' He met her gaze. 'I'd been planning on bringing you breakfast in bed and seeing if you wanted to spend the day together. So when I found out who you were, I felt how you felt. That the whole night was tainted, was a trick, an illusion rather than the magic I'd thought it was.'

She stared at him. 'You wanted to see me, see *Elina* again?' she asked, her voice half a whisper.

'Yes.' It hadn't made sense to him at the time but he'd known that it was what he wanted to happen.

Liyana looked a little shell-shocked. 'The first thing I thought when I woke up that morning was if there was any way I could spend more time with you,' she said softly. 'Even if it meant prolonging the deception.'

'What made it worse for me was wondering if I should have worked it out. Suspected that you were Ashan's sister. After all you explained about your culture, your traditions, should I have seen a family resemblance? You were in the same bar where I was meant to meet Ashan. Maybe I didn't want to know because I knew damn well that even if you had told me who you were it wouldn't have made any difference. Whatever happened between us was too intense, too strong to resist.'

There was a silence and then she blinked. 'I'm glad we talked about this. Somehow, it's made me feel better about what happened and…'

'Put the magic back into that night,' he said softly. There was a silence and all he wanted to do was reignite that magic. Right here. Right now. Jeez, Lorenzo. What was the matter with him? They were putting this behind them. The magic was in the past and it had to remain there.

Liyana was a princess, a grieving widow and his best friend's sister. Three cast-iron reasons why there was no possibility of recasting any sort of spell. Quite simply Lorenzo had nothing to offer except a trick, an illusion, a few hours of physical satisfaction. He knew he wasn't relationship material, knew that he had no understanding of how love worked, or how love should work. After all, love hadn't been a feature in his life. It was something he didn't know how to win and something he had no wish to give. Not when he knew the power it wielded.

More than that, years ago Lorenzo had unwittingly risked losing his friendship with Ashan. No way would he do that again knowingly. It was more than a risk; it was a certainty. Ashan might have accepted Lorenzo as a friend, a true friend, but he would never think Lorenzo was good enough for his sister. Lorenzo knew Ashan had had reservations about Liyana's marriage to Gregor Mertens. It was rare for Ashan to speak of family, but Lorenzo knew his friend's opinion, could remember the words. *'Royalty should marry royalty. We have our own rules and expectations.'*

Ashan would never have paired Lorenzo with Liyana to arrange the wedding ceremony if he had known the truth, known what had happened seven years before. Come to that, he would never have asked Lorenzo to be his best man. But he had and he trusted Lorenzo. Lorenzo wouldn't betray that trust.

'So, we can look back at the memory without anger or awkwardness and put it behind us,' he said firmly. He picked up the remains of his drink. 'To a new start and project wedding.'

A frisson of doubt flitted across her face and then she lifted her glass. 'A new start and project wedding,' she echoed.

CHAPTER THREE

LIYANA OPENED HER eyes and for the first time in a long time she felt a sense of anticipation at the thought of the day ahead. A little buzz, a little tingle, a feeling that the day might hold something unexpected, different…

She gave a small groan. Damn it. The idea of seeing Lorenzo should not make her feel like this. It didn't even make sense; she barely knew the man, but she did know he was not suitable. She had no wish for a 'normal' relationship, one where you went on dates, got to know each other and fell in love. Been there, done that and had a whole designer wardrobe to prove it. Along with a broken heart, cracked and cracked again by the searing humiliations of each of Gregor's infidelities. And whilst tragedy had freed her, her heart was still battle-scarred with wounds she would never be fool enough to risk reopening.

The only relationship she would contemplate would be one that her brain was in complete iron control of. There was no place for her heart or her hormones. Attraction could lead you to make decisions with disastrous consequences. This time if she married it would be for the good of her country, to a man like Prince Luis who would bring tangible benefits to Carathi.

She sighed; with any luck by the end of the day she would be over this odd exhilaration brought on by Lorenzo's presence. Perhaps Lorenzo would prove to be unlikeable, a man with an attractive exterior but undesirable character traits. A man like Gregor.

The reminder of her marriage was enough to drive her to get up and focus on getting ready.

An hour later she pulled her baseball-style sun hat over her ponytail as she climbed out of the car. The plan was to show Lorenzo round Carathi, as part of the cover Ashan had suggested, playing her part as his deputy, and over the next few days she would include some possible wedding venues. Liyana wondered again exactly why Ashan and Kaveesha wanted to do this so fast. She scanned the crowds at the opening to the market, their first port of call.

Her eyes homed in on Lorenzo; then he

turned, saw her and smiled, the impact a laser blast of heat that had nothing to do with the rays of the morning sun. Liyana gritted her teeth and inhaled deeply, wished she could locate the off switch that would at least dial down desire. Forced herself to walk with a measured graceful tread towards him.

'Good morning.' He gestured towards the market. 'This is incredible. I've never seen anywhere so…busy or so vibrant.'

Liyana studied his expression, saw nothing but sincerity on his face, and was aware of a sense of surprise. When she'd brought Gregor to the market he hadn't been able to get away fast enough. Hadn't even wanted to enter the area, had explained, *'I like to see my food on a plate, preferably in a glamorous restaurant. This...just isn't my scene.'* He'd gestured to the market, his lips twisted in something she'd reluctantly identified as distaste. Of course, she'd made excuses for him. Gregor was all about glamour, the market was busy, full, overrun and essentially full of fruit and vegetables and flowers. Which she supposed weren't glamorous. But to her, the market was vital and alive and a thriving part of her culture and traditions.

'It can be overwhelming,' she said now.

Lorenzo shook his head. 'I'm not overwhelmed. But I have to admit I am not a hundred per cent sure what some of this produce is. I'm hoping you'll tell me.'

Liyana blinked.

'Is that OK?'

'Of course it is. I didn't realise this would be your sort of thing.'

He shook his head. 'This is exactly my sort of thing. Food, ingredients, sourcing—they all matter to me. I'm genuinely interested in food; to me it's the heart of my business. Without ingredients there would be no meals.'

'I guess I thought you'd only be interested in the finished product. That's what your business is about, isn't it? Getting the dishes from restaurant to the consumer as fast as possible.' She'd done some research and she knew Lorenzo's company had grown phenomenally fast and was a global household name.

'Yup. Take It Away is a business designed to get food door to door in optimum condition in optimum time. But as I built up the business I became more and more interested in the food itself as well as the logistics of transporting it.'

'I suppose they are sort of intertwined.'

'Exactly, which is why I am excited to go round the market, but as a visitor here I don't understand the rules, if there are any buying or bargaining customs or etiquette. So I am in your hands.'

There was a heartbeat of a pause at his words, and again memories of their night together, the feel of his body under her fingers, the broad sweep of his back, the sculpt of muscle… Liyana bit back a small moan and tried to force her brain into gear.

'Excellent. I will do my best to guide you.' She could feel her whole body heat up and turned away abruptly, hoping he couldn't read her mind. 'Let's go.'

Lorenzo looked behind her. 'I kind of thought you'd have a security guard or something.'

Liyana shook her head. 'It's not the way we work as a royal family. We want to be clear that we are ordinary people and we don't want to use millions of dupends, the national currency,' she clarified, 'of the tax-payers' money every time we set foot out of the door. So we limit security as much as possible.' She started to walk towards the market's entrance. 'Shall we head in?' As they walked, she said, 'To be honest, you are likely to generate more interest than I am. I tend to stay out of the public domain so I am not instantly recognisable to a lot of people. Whereas, although I am working to increase tourism, we don't have masses of Western tourists.'

They entered the portals of the market and as always Liyana breathed deeply, felt absorbed by the hustle and bustle of the crowds, sari-clad women testing fruit, chatting, bargaining, making careful decisions. Baggy-trousered men with long shirts walking alongside, chatting, gossiping, haggling. Street stallholders picking up pre-ordered goods, checking to make sure they'd been given prime-quality produce, the snap and crackle of conversation, good-natured barter and banter, the occasional altercation.

Yet, for once, today all of this felt muted as they walked, by sheer necessity, oh-so close and she was tantalisingly, almost painfully aware of his bulk, the lithe strides he made somehow projecting an aura of strength, almost as if he had designated himself as her bodyguard. As she glanced down all she wanted to do was let her hand accidentally brush his, wanted to close the tiny gap between them even more, wanted…she wasn't even sure what she wanted.

What was wrong with her? She was behaving like an adolescent.

But she couldn't help herself, now she was mesmerised by the sight of his forearm, the swell of muscle, the smattering of hair, his sturdy wrists, the size of his hands, his fingers just the right shape and length and…

Biting her lip, she looked up and saw that he was looking at her, and whatever he'd been saying he broke off and she saw a sudden flare of desire in his eyes as if he could read her mind and, desperately, she sought to recall the conversation, tried to focus on the surroundings, to remind herself of the impossibility of this attraction. Forced her vocal cords to engage with her brain in some sort of meaningful way.

'This market is where many people will pick up the food they need for the day. Many of the population are vegetarian or pescetarian and most people like to eat fresh food every day. Some people even now also don't have the luxury of a fridge or freezer so cooking fresh is a necessity.'

'I've never seen fruit and vegetables so fresh-looking. What are those?'

She followed his gaze to a long winding green vegetable.

'That's snake gourd and, next to it, the one that looks like a prickly green pepper is a bitter gourd. Snake gourds can grow as long as two metres and they smell really strong but actually taste quite bland. But they do make really good chutneys or side dishes if you use lots of spice. The bitter gourd is great in curries. And that there is a jack fruit.'

Lorenzo paused to look at the oval vegetable with its bumpy skin. 'I've tasted jack fruit. It's a big thing in London at the moment but I didn't know they looked like that.'

'It's one of my favourite things,' she said. 'It's technically a fruit but used as a vegetable. And those—' she pointed at a small fruit, dark and velvety-looking '—are gal siyambala or velvet tamarinds.' As she spoke, she relaxed slightly, saw the concentration on his face. 'They are my all-time favourite—they are a bit like eating sour sweets, but in a good-for-you way. Would you like to taste some?'

'Absolutely. I'm also happy to purchase anything I taste. I don't want anyone to be out of pocket.'

Liyana stopped at a stall and smiled at the elderly gentleman behind the array of colourful produce. 'My friend would like to taste a sample of your goods if you are willing to let him?'

The man studied her face and then Lorenzo's. 'I am happy to gift a taste. I would like to show your friend the beauty of what our island produces.'

Turning, Liyana translated and Lorenzo stepped forward and greeted the man in the traditional Carathi way of placing two hands together. Thanked him in a passable attempt at the language.

After that Liyana stood back and acted as translator as the two men spoke. Lorenzo tried a number of fruits and vegetables, asked questions and soon there was a gathering of people all offering advice and recipes. All of which Lorenzo listened to and wrote down before choosing a selection of produce.

'Please tell Viran that I intend to cook the mixed vegetable curry and will return with a report.'

The elderly stall holder smiled an acknowledgement and then, transactions over, they resumed their walk, now carrying a bag full of produce.

'Thank you for translating,' Lorenzo said. 'Sorry for the time it took.'

'There is no need to apologise. You were great.'

He frowned. 'Great in what way? It was a normal conversation.'

'I know. I just meant not all the people I bring here are so natural. Some of them can be condescending. Or they fake an interest.' Including Gregor; not that he'd actually spoken to any of the stallholders, but often his interaction with fans had looked great but it had all been for show, for the camera. Afterwards he'd belittle or laugh at them. But just because Gregor had been like that it didn't mean every wealthy, successful man would be. She gestured to the bag. 'Are you really going to make the recipe?'

'Of course.' Lorenzo glanced at her. 'I don't say things I don't mean. But I could do with a little inspiration. So once we've finished looking round the market I was hoping we could stop at some of the food stalls and try some of the food?'

Another surprise—she'd assumed he'd want to go to some fancy restaurant. 'I would love to buy street food. How about I take you round the flower market and then let's eat?'

The flower market was a revelation in itself, the variety, scents and colours vibrant and alluring. But it wasn't only the flowers or the hazy warmth of the sun that was making this day so memorable. It was Liyana herself. In this setting, seeing her genuine enthusiasm for the produce of her country, hearing how much she knew, the expressive way she moved her hands when making a point, the way she pushed the stray tendrils of hair behind her ear…it was somehow intoxicating, made the world seem a little brighter.

'You need to come here during the flower festival or one of the larger religious festivals. There are flowers everywhere, women wear them in their hair, men wear garlands round their neck and all the temples have displays—the whole island is like a magical, walking botanical experience.'

She broke off and looked up at him. 'What? Do I sound ridiculous?'

'Absolutely not. You sound full of enthusiasm and passion for your country and I'd love to see Carathi during a festival.' He glanced round and then raised a hand. 'Hold on. I have an idea.' He left her side and headed for one of the stalls, returned with a single flower, one that Liyana had identified as a frangipani. 'For you,' he said. 'I thought you could wear it now. Can I?'

She looked up at him, her gaze direct, and then she glanced round at the crowd, none of whom were paying them any attention. Then she nodded and he was aware of a sudden tightening of his chest, told himself this meant nothing. It was simply a gesture, a way of saying a small thank you for the tour. Yet he could see the slight tremble in his fingers as he lifted the bloom and oh-so carefully tucked it behind her ear, threading it through her hair. Making absolutely sure to keep the touch deft, refusing to give into the temptation to linger for even a second longer than necessary.

Yct even the few seconds it took sent heat through him. Her proximity, the silken feel of her hair triggered memories of the feel of that hair against his skin, the cascade flowing through his fingers when he'd released it from its bun all those years ago, the tickle against his chest when she'd slept. And he couldn't help himself; he wondered what would have happened if she really had been Elina Perera, if he had asked to see her again, if…if…if. All impossibilities. They would undoubtedly have split up long ago; no woman would have been able to stick by him. He'd been driven, possessed by the need to succeed.

He stepped back, saw the heat that tinged her cheekbones, heard the catch of her breath and he forced himself to keep his voice bland. 'Perfect,' he said.

'Thank you.' She reached up, touched the flower gently, then took a deep breath and smiled, a smile he recognised as her professional princess smile. 'Now let's eat.'

He followed her out of the market and soon the floral scents were replaced by the tantalising aroma of cooking food; spices sizzled in the sun-warmed air, cumin, coriander and chilli intermingled to weave the promise of culinary delight. He watched as Liyana went from stall to stall, chose a selection of produce and then walked towards a covered area, shaded from the midday heat. Inside were rows of simple square plastic tables and bright red chairs.

They snagged a tray and a table and Liyana quickly opened the paper bags, spread out the food with a satisfied sigh, pointed to each item.

'We'll start with the soup. This is native to Carathi and influenced by so much history. To me it feels symbolic. It's full of simple seafood, crab, prawns and cuttlefish, and this would have been used to nourish sailors and local communities. It's also a fusion of bounty from land and sea, because it's got beans and legumes in it and it is flavoured and thickened with a special flour made from a palm tuber only grown on this island and a few other places in Sri Lanka.' She gestured to the bowl. 'Anyway, enough talking. Try it.'

Lorenzo dipped the spoon in and tasted the soup. 'It's incredible.' The taste was unlike anything he'd had before, an explosion of flavour, the mix and texture of seafood brought out by the tang and taste of the spices, a mixture of heat and bitter and sweet.

Once finished, she gestured to the round doughnut-shaped fritters. 'Deep-fried lentil fritters and coconut chutney. There are so many different recipes for these but these are my favourites. With ginger and green chilli and coriander. They are a staple of Carathi and I love them.'

Lorenzo bit into one and grinned at her. 'Consider me a fan,' he said. 'I could keep on eating them.'

She returned the smile then looked down at the food contemplatively. 'I wouldn't have the first idea how to transport food like this from door to door. How *do* you deliver food so that it stays fresh?'

'It isn't possible to keep it perfect over longer distances, though I do my best. Our transport has special temperature and equipment and I use containers made of different materials from the usual takeout boxes. You do pay a bit more for delivery by Take It Away but I have done my best to eradicate cold, soggy takeaway pizza, lukewarm curries and falling-apart sandwiches. I also pay my delivery drivers properly and don't expect them to risk life and limb. I know what that feels like.'

'You were a delivery driver?'

'Yup. It was one of my jobs whilst I was a student. In fact, it's how I became friends with Ashan.'

'Tell me.'

'I was delivering food to one of his parties. Pizzas. They were already not at their best when I picked them up but the restaurant didn't care. I tried to get there as fast as I could but traffic was awful. One of his friends answered the door and I couldn't really blame him for giving me a hard time but he was getting a bit offensive. Your brother came over, laid into him and threw him out. Then we got talking and it turned out we were in the same university and in the same year. We ended up friends.'

Lorenzo could hear the remembered surprise in his voice. At first, he'd been sure that Ashan's friendship wasn't real, that it was an example of a prince slumming it, the novelty factor. A view he knew was shared by most of Ashan's other friends. But Ashan had proved him wrong, had stuck around and as they'd met in the library, got talking, they'd realised that despite their different backgrounds they'd liked each other. And that had been a novelty for Lorenzo. A friendship based on mutual liking, no conditions or confusing swings. A friendship he would never imperil again.

'I guess we just clicked. And Ashan had my back. When he could see I needed time to study he'd step in for me.'

'Ashan delivered pizzas?'

'Yes. He also covered a couple of my shifts in the student bar so I could study. I think he'd have preferred to give or loan me money, but when I refused that he insisted on taking over some of my shifts. I owe him; he's never asked anything from me. Until now.'

'That's why it's so important to you.'

'Yes. I know I wasn't exactly the sort of person Ashan usually made friends with. I didn't fit in his social circle but he didn't mind.' And he'd accepted Lorenzo. 'I've never felt there was something I could do for him. Till now.'

'Ashan would have valued the fact that you wouldn't accept money from him. It is hard sometimes for royalty to make true friends because we always worry if people are with us for our title. Ashan knows you are the real thing. And I understand now why he wanted you to be his best man.'

'Rather than a more political choice?'

'Yes. There were some people who felt he should choose someone more qualified.'

'By birth?' The irony almost made him laugh. Almost. Because his birth father had been upper class, heir to a thriving Tuscan wine estate that had been in business for centuries, passing from son to son. But upper class or not it had turned out Roberto was just as much of a dastard as Matt.

Roberto had been married when he'd slept with Lorenzo and Daisy's mother. And as soon as he'd learnt of the pregnancy Roberto had vanished, had left their mother high and dry.

Perhaps Ashan's friends wouldn't care about that, would believe that his class justified his actions. Well, Lorenzo disagreed. As far as he was concerned Roberto was as bad in his own way as Matt. If not worse. Matt had at least given parenthood a chance. It was another reason not to get involved with the Rossis; he wasn't sure he wanted anything to do with a lifestyle, a heritage, that Roberto had clearly wanted to exclude him from. The Rossi vineyard was Amara's by blood and right. Lorenzo didn't want to be part of it, something that he would never feel entitled to for real. Just as he'd never been entitled to Matt's love.

'Lorenzo?'

He looked across, saw the concern in Liyana's eyes and for a ridiculous instant he was tempted to ask her opinion, tell her the truth. Explain that a few months ago Daisy had found some letters in a box in their parents' attic. Letters smudged with his mother's tears, letters that made it plain Matt was not their father. Ask her what to do about Vittorio, about Amara, about the Rossi blood that ran in his veins.

But of course he wouldn't tell Liyana. He and Daisy hadn't even told their mother that they knew the truth. Lorenzo had agreed to let Daisy make that decision; after all it was Daisy who was close to Matt, it was Daisy who was closer to their mother, and he respected her right to make the call.

He shook his head in apology. 'Sorry. I was thinking.'

'There is no need to apologise. I should be doing that. I didn't mean to offend you or imply Ashan is regretting his choice or…'

'I know that.' Lorenzo summoned a smile of

reassurance, brought himself back to the present. 'Truly. I know damn well Ashan wouldn't do anything he didn't want to. But if politics means he has to change his mind I would understand. But no matter what, I want to help him with this ceremony.' He ate the last piece of the tangy, spicy lentil fritter. 'So where next?'

CHAPTER FOUR

'HERE IS NEXT,' Liyana said as they alighted from the car at the ornate gateway to a large public park. 'This way.' She led the way along the well-maintained pathways that meandered under the shade of sprawling, ancient trees, massive-trunked mahogany, tamarind and mango that scented the air, past a pond and beds of carefully tended flowers, buzzing with insects and butterflies.

'This is actually one of my favourite places on the island. It used to belong to the royal family, but my grandmother handed it over to the public. Ashan and I used to come here a lot as children and now it's a place where I come to think and I know Ashan does too.'

She led the way around a corner and stopped, turned to Lorenzo and saw the look of astonishment and awe and appreciation as he took in the two buildings in front of them. A temple and a church side by side.

'This sort of symbolises the beliefs and traditions of our culture or our people. We are a place where temples and churches do literally live side by side. Neither this temple nor this church are the most lavish or maybe even the most beautiful on Carathi but they symbolise our history and our spirituality.'

'This feels like a place of peace,' he said quietly as they contemplated the two buildings. The temple was a vibrant low-roofed amalgamation, awash with arches, panelled in gold, with turquoise mosaics depicting the stories and legends of the god it was dedicated to. Next door, the church was a stark contrast, with its symmetrical white stone walls and stained-glass windows and the towering bell tower that spired up to the azure blue of the sky as if it could pierce the clouds. Yet somehow both the colourful and the monotone worked together to create a sense of unity.

'One of the things I am most proud of about our kingdom is that different religions coexist in harmony, a place of tolerance where we are all citizens together. It helps, I think, that different religions have been established for so long and neither one nor the other is richer or poorer.'

They walked as she spoke and came to a

mosaicked courtyard with various vendors dotted around the edges. 'Coffee?' she asked.

'That sounds good.' And soon they were sitting on the tree-shaded lawn, drinks in hand.

'So, the class system isn't religion-based?' he asked.

'Exactly. Having said that, we are far from perfect. There is way too much poverty in our land and that is something I am hoping we can address by increasing tourism and investment in Carathi. For cxample, the market: I love it and I know you did too but it's not enough as it is to really draw tourists in. They can't buy a snake gourd to take back home with them. We need other stalls at the market, textiles, souvenirs, other products that are native to our culture.

'I want to invest money in encouraging women to work, to start businesses making things. I want to persuade overseas investors to build hotels, I want more restaurants. More places like the Chandraya Bar. That is a brilliant example of local initiative. I mean, one of my ideas was to install the eating area where we sat; I thought it would increase street-food sales. The vendors pay the owner a small percentage of sales. I don't want to lose our authenticity; I don't simply want to become a tourist mecca but I want more people to come here, to know about us.'

She knew her parents had hoped that Gregor would help with that, but he hadn't. He hadn't felt comfortable here; at first, he had enjoyed being quasi-royal, enjoyed living in a palace. But once he'd realised how hard her parents worked, realised that the royals were not overly interested in opulence or luxury, he'd lost interest. So he hadn't wanted to visit and had made it clear that he felt a wife should be by her husband's side or not complain if he found solace elsewhere.

But Liyana had missed her country with a fierceness that had almost hurt and now she was back she wanted to make up for her previous absence, passionately wanted to make a difference. In whatever way she could—which was why she was considering the marriage to Prince Luis. It would bring good to Carathi, be the act of a true princess who understood what was due from royalty and loyalty to country.

'I want Carathi to be a more prosperous place where our people can thrive, where education improves, where poverty is lessened…' She broke off. 'Sorry. There is no reason you should be remotely interested in this.'

'I am interested. Ashan never really discussed here much; I'm not sure why.'

'I think he has always been worried about people taking his words and twisting them in some way. He has always been taught to be wary of people, to keep things to himself.'

'That makes sense but I promise I am interested. Curious about the place my best friend grew up in, and listening to you, hearing your enthusiasm…that makes me want to hear more too.'

'Really?' Liyana couldn't help the question. The idea that she was interesting made her feel a little warm and fuzzy and chuffed.

'Really.' His deep voice held warmth and a smile and slid over her skin.

'OK. Basically, we are a small island, with the potential to be a prosperous one. We have beautiful beaches, the sea is warm and clean and the weather mostly ranges from warm to very hot whatever the season, which is obviously a draw for visitors. The only drawback is, because of where we are located, we do sometimes have freak tropical storms. The truly scary kind that spring out of nowhere, wreak damage and then leave as if they have never been.

'Also, we lack infrastructure. So there is

nowhere for people to stay other than a few campsites and guest houses. And a couple of more upmarket hotels in the city centre. There are, though, plenty of things to see and do. In terms of our history, we've always been ruled by a monarchy and it has mostly been very successful. But recently there was civil unrest and that has undoubtedly taken our island backwards. There are cities and towns that are still ravaged and it has also made people uneasy. Given us a reputation of danger.'

'What happened?'

'My grandfather was a man who believed royalty was divine; he was a tyrant. Scandal followed scandal, he married more times than I can count, every wedding a splendid, lavish affair. There were wild parties, illegitimate children, a jet-set lifestyle and he spent a fortune on extending the palace. To pay for it he raised taxes. There was very nearly civil war. Uprisings, violence, all put down by his security forces.'

Liyana paused but she could see that he was really listening, as if he could picture the scenes.

'Go on.'

'Then he met my grandmother. She was beautiful, intelligent and politically astute.

She made a deal with him. If he married her, she'd sort out his problems and, more than that, she'd make him happy. And she did. I remember her and she was an incredible woman; she was calm and serene and yet she had a steeliness to her. But she was also kind and wise; my grandfather listened to her, curbed his excesses. They had a child, an heir, my father. And my grandmother made sure he understood his duties and how to rule.

'My grandfather died when my father was still a child and my grandmother ruled as regent; the country was still on the brink but she brought it back and my parents are continuing her good work. But it's why the royal family has to be squeaky clean, and completely scandal-free. That was drummed into Ashan and me from the start.'

'Ashan threw a few parties, had a few girlfriends.'

'Sure, but it is different for him. He's a man; a prince is allowed to "sow a few wild oats". That doesn't count as scandal. A princess putting even a foot wrong is a scandal. Ashan is a natural; he knows exactly how to get the balance right. I never have. It was always a struggle for me. I didn't like the rules and regulations, the restrictions.'

She'd never been a naturally good princess. Until now, when she was doing work that she believed mattered, when, finally, she was doing good for her country. A good that she could continue by marrying Prince Luis. Settling into a safe marriage with a good man, having a family and doing good for Carathi. Learning to live within the boundaries, playing by the rules.

'Surely that is natural,' he said now, his tone gentle. 'And it sounds to me as though, however much you didn't like them, you didn't actually *do* anything scandalous.'

He was right. She hadn't done anything scandalous as such. But in marrying Gregor she hadn't played by the rules. She'd done what she'd wanted in the name of love and romance. The marriage had not done her country any good and once Gregor's infidelities had started she had spent every moment staving off scandal.

Memories flooded her, of the humiliations she'd endured in order to keep scandal from the door, the constant stress of waiting for Gregor's infidelities to be found out, the actual pain of smiling as she'd played the devoted wife. She'd tried to rekindle the dream of love and romance that seemed to have slipped through her fingers in a dwindle of dust and ashes. Yet Gregor had told her he did love her, messed with her head and her heart as she'd tried to rewrite the rules of love. But scandal *had* been avoided. The marriage had ended by death rather than divorce. Liyana shivered slightly, rammed again with the guilty knowledge that it was death that had freed her.

Seeing that Lorenzo was looking at her with dawning concern, she managed a smile. 'Sometimes I think it was more through luck than judgement, but hopefully both Ashan and I will continue to avoid scandal. Right now, I am focused on my remit, which is to increase tourism. That's why my parents have made me a royal advisor to the minister of tourism.'

'Why not make you the actual minister of tourism?' he asked. 'I can hear how passionate you are about your country and it sounds like you have plenty of ideas. Good, effective ideas. Or at least a deputy minister.'

Liyana shook her head. 'It doesn't work like that here. Especially for royalty. My father is the ruler. Ashan is the heir. My mother, me, Kaveesha... We are helpers, advisors...not decision makers.'

'In essence your father is the CEO and your mother helps but he has the final say.'

She realised he was quoting her words from seven years ago and she felt heat touch her cheeks. 'Yup.'

'So the minister will have the final say on your ideas and he doesn't have to take your advice?'

'Yes, even though…' Liyana bit the words back, remembered the golden rule of discretion.

Lorenzo studied her face. 'I am making a wild guess here. You do all the work and he takes all the credit.'

It was a fair assessment but she wouldn't admit it. She'd learnt from the past, learnt to appreciate what she did have. Learnt not to trust. Sure, Lorenzo seemed like a good man, sure, Ashan trusted him, but at the end of the day Liyana had believed in Gregor, believed he'd loved her for herself, believed he was a good man. And she'd got it all wrong.

'I don't mind the work. I truly don't. Plus, my royal status does sometimes help, makes people more open to investment in the country. And whatever the title is I feel like I am making a difference and that's what I wanted, what I needed after…after I returned to Carathi.'

There was a silence and she sensed Lorenzo

shift his weight on the seat. He looked towards the temple and then turned back to her.

'I'm sorry, Liyana, sorry for your loss and sorry I have not said this before. I sensed that perhaps you prefer people not to talk about it, but I am sorry you lost your husband. I cannot imagine the grief.'

The words were simple but she heard the sincerity behind them and they moved her, even as, for the first time in the two years sincc Gregor's death, she wanted to refute them. Wanted to explain that, yes, she grieved, but not in the way he imagined. Not in the way the whole world thought. She pressed her lips together; she couldn't tell him, didn't even understand why she wanted to. Her grief, her marriage, her guilt—all were things she needed to keep close to herself.

'Thank you,' she said. 'His death was a tragedy, not only for me, but for his family and all his fans. There was such an outpouring of grief from all over the world, people who felt as if they knew him.'

'That must have made it even harder for you. Your loss was the greatest; your world must have upturned; you lost the future you believed you had.'

Now guilt really did hit. Because she had

lost a future she hadn't wanted. A future where her choices had been stark. Remain in a miserable marriage of her own making, cut off from home and family. Or leave Gregor and cause a scandal that would impact her country.

Liyana closed her eyes, blocked out the memories she was usually so adept at keeping at bay. Had to keep at bay in order to play the part she had vowed to play.

Opening her eyes, she forced a small smile to her face. 'It was hard, but I know how much Gregor would have appreciated his fans' grief. He adored the attention, loved the lifestyle his position brought him.' That much was the truth. Gregor had enjoyed every moment of his life, had never let himself worry about anything or anyone other than himself.

Lorenzo studied her expression. 'I am so sorry, Liyana. I didn't mean to remind you of what you lost. I truly am sorry.'

She could hear that he really was and the idea caused further mixed emotions. She wasn't used to people caring. Gregor hadn't cared if she was upset; had seen it as 'her problem', or a flaw in Liyana.

'It's OK,' she said. 'Really it is.' She managed a proper princess smile. 'I am here, I enjoy what I do and I am happy to work in the background, to get on with it without being noticed.'

'I find it hard to believe that you aren't noticed.'

'Believe it. It's an art. It's all in your clothes and make-up and how you present yourself. I am an expert at fading into the background.'

'But why do you want to fade into the background?'

'I prefer to be invisible; I truly believe I get more done.' Plus, it felt safer; if she was in the background she couldn't do anything stupid or impulsive, could play her role more easily. 'And what I do matters to me.'

'I can hear how much you care and how dedicated you are.'

She tipped her head to one side. 'I'm sensing a but…'

'It isn't a but. I am glad that, after what happened to you, you have found purpose and a cause. But don't let work subsume you. I completely understand that work and doing something worthwhile that you love must help you cope with your loss but…don't lose who you are.'

'What do you mean?' Perhaps she should end this conversation but, somehow, she couldn't. The idea that he was interested in her as a person was almost intoxicating, impossible to close down, even though she sensed she should. Since her marriage she'd kept everyone at arm's length. Yet somehow Lorenzo had managed to get past her initial defences, making it hard for her to keep her guard up, her princess mask in place.

'I mean you are the person who enjoyed a glamorous lifestyle and you were once a young woman who wanted to escape some of the rules and restrictions. Don't lose that person. You don't always have to stick to the rules; if you are doing the work, if you are putting in the hours, then the credit should be yours. Maybe you shouldn't fade into the background for ever. I get the future you believed you were going to have was wrenched away but that doesn't mean you should fade into obscurity.'

There was a silence and then she leant forward and without thinking she reached up and gently touched his cheek with the palm of her hand. And froze. The sensation that ran through her was liquid heat through her veins; the rough stubble under her fingers, the proximity of him, the masculine scent, it all dizzied her. Along with the warmth that came of someone thinking about her, caring enough to give real advice based on what they believed was right for her rather than what they believed she should do for the good of others or the good of her country.

'Thank you,' she said softly and, suddenly oh-so aware of their surroundings, she dropped her hand, looked round hurriedly, prayed they hadn't been spotted. 'And now I think it's time to move on.'

He looked as shell-shocked as she did but he nodded. 'Agreed, but thank you for bringing me here and for showing me the market this morning.' He glanced at his watch. 'I know you have a meeting this afternoon, but I was wondering if you and Ashan and Kaveesha would like to come to dinner with me this evening? I could cook the curry that Viran and all the other people at the market suggested and we could maybe have a chat with them for a bit more detail on what they want.'

'Aren't you staying in a hotel?' she asked.

He shook his head. 'Ashan offered me the use of one of his royal residences. Actually, he didn't offer, he insisted. So I'm happy to cook for all of us and there is no chance of us being overheard.'

'That sounds great. I'll check in with Ashan

and we'll see you this evening. I'm looking forward to it and seeing the fruits of your labour.'

And, heaven help her, she really was.

CHAPTER FIVE

LORENZO EYED THE pot of bubbling food on the hob, stirred the contents and inhaled the tangy aroma, admitting that he was hoping to impress Liyana. Which he acknowledged to be ridiculous. She'd been married to Gregor, had eaten in the best restaurants in the world, she was hardly likely to rate his efforts.

Yet somehow it was hard to equate that woman with the one who'd enjoyed street food, discussed her work with such passion and been content sipping coffee in a park. Hard to understand her desire for invisibility. Except to put it down to grief, because Lorenzo had seen the shadows in her eyes when she'd discussed her marriage, seen pain and sadness.

Her whole life with Gregor had been one of glamour and it must be hard not to associate glamour and enjoyment and being visible with the loss she had endured. Lorenzo tried to imagine that loss, knew that now he had some understanding of how much she must be grieving he *had* to clamp down on attraction. Because this glimpse into her loss had shown him that what Liyana had experienced with her husband was something Lorenzo could never offer or even fathom. Her love for Gregor had meant she had chosen to leave a country she clearly loved, to break with tradition and marry a non-royal. And that meant that that love must have been something out of the ordinary.

In comparison he could see how tawdry what he could offer was. Attraction without commitment, without love. That was tawdry *and* inadequate. And Lorenzo understood his own inadequacy all too well. He hadn't been an adequate son: Matt had despised him, found him worthy of nothing but contempt. His mum claimed to love him and Lorenzo clung to that claim like a drowning man clung to a lifeline. Yet she had tacitly agreed with Matt's treatment of him, stayed in the marriage despite that treatment, told Lorenzo it was down to him to try harder. And so, she had implied, the inadequacy was his.

An inadequacy Lorenzo had accepted as truth, the belief bolstered by the way Daisy was loved by both Matt and Karen, the knowledge he didn't measure up to his sister, that Daisy held a magic key that unlocked love. A key Lorenzo did not possess and couldn't earn.

He understood that, knew love was not for him, wouldn't even try to measure up to Gregor Mertens. Yet…he wanted to help. He'd sensed somehow that, along with invisibility, Liyana had also kept herself isolated, was dealing with her loss alone. Had thrown herself into work. Yet there was no way he could question her commitment to that work; he had been thoroughly impressed with her ideas and her vision. Which was why he was planning to discuss some investment ideas with her and Ashan and Kaveesha over dinner if there was time.

A knock at the door interrupted his thought process and he went to open it, saw Ashan and Liyana on the doorstep.

'Kaveesha is going to join us soon,' Ashan said, and Lorenzo glanced at his friend, heard an edge to his tone, saw his expression was tinged with worry.

He glanced at Liyana, who gave the smallest of shrugs as Ashan's phone beeped. Ashan glanced down.

'I am really sorry. I've got to go. Kaveesha's not feeling great. If I can I'll come back. Otherwise, I trust you both to come up with a perfect ceremony—surprise us.'

A few seconds later the back door slammed and Ashan was gone.

Lorenzo turned to Liyana. 'What was that about?' he asked.

'Kaveesha did look a little pale when I saw her earlier. I guess Ashan wants to look after her. I suppose when you're in love you also turn into a ministering angel.'

'Well, until he does come back it's just the two of us,' he said.

There was a silence and the words seemed to reverberate around the room.

'Yes,' she said and he could hear a soupçon of doubt in her voice.

'If you think people will be scandalised or if it will start up rumours, then of course you should go. But Ashan may come back, and this *would* be a good opportunity to discuss the ceremony. *And* I have a whole vat of food that needs eating.'

He could still see indecision on her face, as if she was conducting some sort of inner argument with herself.

'But it's up to you. I get that you understand how people will think.'

'No. You're right. It's fine. I'll stay. We do need to talk.'

Liyana inhaled the aroma of the food and smiled. 'And the curry does smell great and I am hungry.'

'Then let's eat.' Within minutes he'd assembled everything on the table in the kitchen. 'I did my best to follow the recipe but I have had to improvise a little. And I had a little help. Rosa, the lovely lady who Ashan insisted come in to check on me and look after the place, took pity on me and gave me some advice.'

'Rosa is lovely,' Liyana said. 'I've known her all my life. You must have impressed her. Rosa usually disapproves of Ashan's overseas friends. She thinks they lead him astray.'

Liyana served herself, waited for him to do the same and then forked up a mouthful. 'This is fantastic. Just the right amount of zing but not so much that the vegetables are overpowered. And the vegetables are the exact right texture as well. So, I'm impressed on all fronts. You won Rosa over and this is delicious.'

Warmth touched him at her genuine appreciation. 'Maybe I could cook it for Ashan and Kaveesha as a celebratory meal after the ceremony? I'm assuming we won't be able to go to a restaurant, but it would be nice to have some sort of "reception". Also, what sort of ceremony are we arranging? Is it the equivalent of a register office?'

'It's a bit complicated. The most important thing about a Carathi wedding is the ceremony that accompanies it. It's based on traditions going back years and is conducted on a wooden platform decorated in a way that is personal to the couple to show the hope for their future life together. It is usually overseen by a religious elder and it is very family based.'

'But they don't want your family to know about it.'

'No,' Liyana agreed. 'So all we can do is make it as meaningful as we can. We need to find a private place and I can find a celebrant, and I will have to trust one person, a friend of mine, to carry out the legal side of it.'

'Once we find a place I'll work out the practicalities, but I'm not really a romance expert so I'll make sure to run it all past you.'

'I'm not sure I qual—' Liyana broke off.

'I'm sorry,' he said. 'All of this must be reminding you of your own wedding and bringing back memories. I know it must be hard, so please tell me if there is anything you would rather leave to me.'

'Truly, I'm good. I am happy to do this for Ashan because I am truly happy for him and Kaveesha and to see them so happy now.'

'So he wasn't happy before?'

Liyana served herself a second helping and then shook her head. 'No. It's not that. But I don't think Ashan ever thought he'd fall in love; he always knew that as heir he would have to marry for duty. Make an alliance. His marriage would always be political and he always accepted that. I think it's why he never believed in love.'

Lorenzo nodded, refrained from explaining he thoroughly endorsed the view. As far as he could see, love got you precisely nowhere. Worse, it took you into a territory where you gave someone else power over you. Just as his mother had done with her husband. No matter how Matt treated her she refused to leave because they 'loved' each other.

It was a stance he could not understand. Matt had blown hot and cold, made the whole family dance to his tune, all in the name of love. Everyone twirling, whirling, all striving to win his approval and affection. Daisy moulded into an eternal keeper of the peace, rewarded by Matt's love, but always feeling guilty because that love was withheld from her twin. Lorenzo desperate to win Matt's love and all the time trying not to resent Daisy. Because he did love his sister and even if Lorenzo couldn't win even liking from Matt, he would have hated his sister to suffer in the same way he had. And he admired Daisy for her ability to love and stand by her brother without antagonising Matt. But it had been an added torment for Lorenzo, seeing that his father was capable of love and affection. But not for him.

And his mother constantly trying, trying to fulfil all the tasks, tick all the boxes. Getting up early to put her make-up on, keeping the house sparkling clean without so much as a crumb on the perfectly polished kitchen counters, beer at the right temperature ready to pour whenever Matt walked through the door. And all of this done for what? The reward of a smile, a word of approval. A period of peace, a cessation of insults and put-downs.

But those were few and far between, doled out with the parsimony of a miser. The rest of the time, his mother's face held worry, fear, a careworn expression that tore at Lorenzo's heart, made him unable to blame his mother for not defending him. When the price she would pay would be so high and yield so little.

There was no way he would give anyone that

sort of power over him; love clearly clouded judgement and caused you to make foolish decisions. As for being loved, he didn't want to wield that sort of power over anyone either. Wasn't sure he could promise never to hurt another person.

'But now Ashan does believe in love?' he asked, tried and knew he'd failed to keep the scepticism from his voice.

'It looks like it. The marriage was arranged but of course our parents and Kaveesha's wouldn't have forced them into it if they didn't like each other. They met and they decided they could make it work and somewhere along the line liking changed and grew into love. I have never seen Ashan like this; the way he looks at her, how protective he is. I mean, look at him today…' She glanced at him and gave a sudden grin. 'You really aren't looking impressed at all.'

Lorenzo shrugged. 'If Ashan is happy, of course I am happy for him…'

'I sense a but.'

'Love isn't really my thing… But if I was in Ashan's position, I'd prefer an arranged marriage.'

'Why?'

'Ashan is going to be a ruler, and I know he

wants to rule wisely and well. Love can complicate that. It has a power of its own. A power that muddles your mind, makes you make illogical or even bad decisions because you can't see clearly. It clouds your vision.'

'I think Ashan would say that it brings sunshine.'

'The kind that beats down on you and makes you dizzy and weak,' Lorenzo said.

'So speaks a true cynic.'

'Absolutely.' Lorenzo pushed his plate away. 'But that is how I feel personally. I promise I will still do my best for Ashan and Kaveesha and I truly do hope it works out for them. I will do nothing to undermine their belief and dreams.'

'Even if you think they are deluded.'

'Even if.' He tried to read her expression, sensed she was guarding a thought.

'You truly don't believe in love?'

'Never have, never will. Or at least not for me.'

'So you've never been in love?'

'No.'

'But you must have had relationships?'

'Not really.' He shrugged, wanting to explain his stance to her. Perhaps setting out his views would somehow help firefight their attraction, remind him that it could go nowhere. 'When I was younger, I was completely focused on succeeding, on making my business idea work. There wasn't time for relationships. Any woman I met pretty soon ran a mile. I can't say I blame them. I was working three jobs and what little spare time I had I was sitting on a laptop making spreadsheets and business plans.'

'They could have helped,' Liyana said.

'Even if they'd wanted to, I don't think I wanted help.' It had been important, vital to him that this was his success, that his father would have to acknowledge his success alone. 'Live by the sword, die by the sword. That was pretty much my motto.'

'It sounds as though you were driven. That success was essential.'

'Yes.'

'But you've achieved that now. So surely you have time for relationships?'

He shrugged. 'There still isn't a lot of time. My last relationship was a couple of years ago. That lasted about a year.'

'That sounds long term to me.'

'It was and it wasn't. We didn't see each other that often. She was very career orientated as well so we'd meet every so often, the occasional weekend away, a dinner here, a dinner there. It was more about…'

'Sex,' Liyana supplied and then looked aghast. 'Sorry. I can't believe I even said that. I mean, I really can't.'

'Hey. It's OK. You don't have to be polite or observe the rules of etiquette tonight. It's just you and me.' There was a silence as the atmosphere heightened. The two of them. No one else. No hustle and bustle of crowds, no fellow diners or staff, no Ashan, no Kaveesha. No one at all. Aware of the tension in the air, in his jaw, in his shoulders, he tried to focus on the conversation, to be clinical. 'I can see why you would say that. But it was more than that—we enjoyed each other's company out of the bedroom as well. But…when we were apart, we didn't really think about each other.'

'And that was what you wanted.'

'Yes, that was what we both wanted. It was uncomplicated and enjoyable and it suited us both.'

'What happened?'

'She wanted to open the relationship up. For us both to be free to date other people. She said it made sense. We were apart a lot and we weren't emotionally committed in any way. I understood where she was coming from but it wouldn't have worked for me. I declined and we parted ways amicably.'

Liyana stared at him. 'You passed up an opportunity to multi-date?'

'Yes.' Lorenzo frowned. 'You sound surprised. Don't you believe in fidelity?'

Liyana looked away from him and then back and her voice sounded a little forced. 'Of course I do. Just, given she obviously didn't want or expect it, I thought most men would be happy with the idea.'

'Then maybe I'm not most men. I may not believe in love or even long-term commitment, but I can offer fidelity.' Maybe because it was all he could offer. 'I hope my views haven't offended you.'

'Why would they?'

'I know that your marriage was one of the most publicised romance stories of our time.'

Liyana raised a hand and Lorenzo was mesmerised by the sheer grace of the movement, studied the slender fingers, and a memory jolted, those same fingers on his skin, and he forced his expression to remain neutral, felt his jaw clench with the effort.

'You have to stop apologising,' she said now. 'We are going to spend time together over the next few days and we are planning a wedding.

You can't keep saying sorry or worry you've upset me. My feelings, my grief, they… I've learnt to live with them as best I can.'

Her voice was heavy and something twisted in his chest, a desire to somehow lighten her load, make her a little bit happy even if he didn't know how. How could you lift the grief of loss? Another reason not to love, surely.

He met her gaze and saw something in her brown eyes, a pain that he couldn't pinpoint, but that she was feeling pain, he didn't doubt, and without thinking he reached out and covered her hand with his own. And there it was, the zing that they had both agreed to fight, and yet right here and now he didn't want to fight it. Sensed she didn't want sympathy, and all he wanted to do right now was distract her, give her some joy, some happiness and, even though he knew it wasn't right, he wanted to lean across and kiss her. Knew that by doing so he would and could wipe away the sadness temporarily. And what harm could there be in a kiss?

Their eyes met and he could see the desire in hers, wondered if she craved contact as much as he did. Wondered if she wanted a momentary obliteration of grief. Surely there was no harm in that.

Then somehow, as if their minds had indeed travelled the same path, their bodies seemed to find the same synchronicity and they were leaning closer, oh, so much closer and so close he could see the impossible length of her lashes, the tiny birthmark at the side of her mouth.

The air seemed to sizzle and he knew the momentum had gone too far, was impossible to stop, and then his lips met hers and all coherent thought stopped as blind instinct took over.

It felt so inevitable, so right. Her lips felt new and yet familiar and oh-so glorious. His hands cupped her face, and she gave a small gasp of pleasure as he deepened the kiss and sensations volted through him, pleasure, desire and a yearning for more. The taste of her, the feel of her and now a need to be closer, one she felt too, and in one seamless movement they rose so they were standing, still locked together but now her body was pressed against his, her hand looped round his neck, and there was nothing in the world except her and him and this moment.

Until with almost comic timing both their phones beeped in synchronicity, the sound bursting the bubble with a knell of reality, and she jumped backwards abruptly, put a hand out to steady herself and caught the side of her glass and it toppled to one side, the remnants of her wine trickling onto the table.

Instantly she righted the glass and stared at him, wide-eyed, as the last ember of desire faded to a panic-stricken cloud. 'I'll go get a cloth,' she said and she was gone, leaving Lorenzo frozen, full of spiralling emotions where relief and regret mingled and fought. He told himself relief should be paramount—if their phones hadn't intervened, they would still be entwined in an embrace, caught in the flames of desire and he had no idea what would have happened next.

CHAPTER SIX

LIYANA TOOK A deep breath as she looked round the kitchen and found a roll of kitchen towel. Saw the evidence that Lorenzo had indeed made the meal from scratch and further evidence that he tidied away after himself. Her mind taking the details in in an attempt to bring her heart rate under control, to block out the sheer foolishness of what she had just done.

What had she been thinking? Clearly, she hadn't been thinking at all. She closed her eyes, resisted the urge to thump the marble counter. Two and a half years of being in control, making herself into the dutiful princess she wished she had always been, keeping her counsel, being a grieving widow, pretending her marriage had been the romantic idyll everyone believed it to be. She had done nothing impulsive, had stayed in the background and she'd worked hard, achieved things she was proud of.

And now a few hours with Lorenzo Cavendish and she'd ended up in his arms, enjoying, *revelling* in a kiss that had dizzied her, awakened a desire that still roiled and clenched her tummy and had taken her to soaring heights of pleasure. But the problem with soaring heights was they could be succeeded by a plummeting fall.

Liyana realised she was holding the roll of kitchen towel so hard she was crushing it. She took a deep breath, forced herself to check her phone to see who the message had been from. The message that had saved them from that kiss. It was Ashan, telling them that he wouldn't be back. So what to do now? She could leave but that was the coward's way out. And it wasn't fair; this wasn't Lorenzo's fault. Even if she did leave, she would have to see him the next day. They still had a ceremony to arrange.

So she would do the right thing. She would go in there and bring things under control.

She picked up the kitchen towel and returned to the dining area only to find he'd used the napkins to wipe up the few drops of wine, had stacked their dirty plates and was standing by the window looking out at the walled mosaic patio.

He turned as she came in.

'I apologise,' he said, the words direct and clear; she could see the tension in his jaw. 'I thought…' He made a gesture with his hands. 'I hoped to distract you from your grief, but that should never have happened. I didn't expect…'

He hadn't expected a kiss to get so out of hand, to be so all-consuming, so right, so overwhelming. She got that.

'You don't need to apologise. There were two of us in it and the blame is as much mine. More so, in fact, because I have more to lose.' She gestured to the armchairs. 'Perhaps we should sit.'

He nodded, waited for her to choose which chair she wanted then sat opposite her.

She took a deep breath, knew she had to explain why she *couldn't* kiss him like that again. Tell him and remind herself. She'd thought she could control this attraction through sheer willpower, by knowing it was impossible. Turned out that wasn't enough.

'I told you earlier how important it is for my life to be scandal-free. That kiss was a risk I should never have taken. Anyone could have come in. Ashan and Kaveesha could have walked in on us. Rosa could have come in to help with dinner. A lurking reporter could have walked by and taken a photo.' The very idea had her clenching her hand around the leather of the arm rest. 'If any of those things had happened it would cause a massive problem. It would take away everything I've worked for—instead of being taken seriously as someone working for my country's good, it would be all about "Widowed princess caught in arms of brother's best man".' How could she have been so foolish? To her own annoyance she could feel tears prickle the backs of her eyelids.

She took a deep breath, realised too that Lorenzo must think she'd lost the plot, was being ridiculously melodramatic.

'Liyana. It's OK.' But instead of derision she saw concern in his dark blue eyes as he leant forward as if to offer comfort and then instantly moved back again. Concern, apology, guilt, and a bit of confusion. 'I know you explained earlier but I don't think I fully understood the true implications. I didn't realise a kiss could have such a significant consequence. I truly am sorry.'

His acceptance, his understanding, the sincerity of his apology, the gentleness of his voice made the tears threaten again. 'There is no need for you to apologise. It's on me.'

'No. You said it yourself. There were two of us in it and you had told me about your culture, the expectations a princess bears. I should have taken that on board. But don't be so hard on yourself. You're human and sometimes human emotions, feelings, get the better of us.'

She shook her head. 'It's not that easy.'

'Why not?'

Liyana looked at him, wanted to explain what was fully at stake here. But more than that, she wanted to confide in him. Share some part of her life, who she was with him. Secure in the instinctive knowledge that she could trust him, the idea novel and one she should perhaps be wary of. Yet, surely, he deserved to completely understand the damage that their attraction could cause, the domino effect it could have.

'It's complicated,' she said. 'But I think it's only fair that you should know.' She managed a small smile. 'I may get a little more wine, if that's OK.'

'I'll get it.' He rose to his feet and Liyana forced herself not to focus on the lithe muscular grace of his movements. Turned away to marshal her thoughts.

* * *

Lorenzo poured the wine with a sense of warmth that Liyana was choosing to confide in him. He sensed that it wasn't easy for her to trust; trust didn't come easily to him either, maybe because from birth he had been unable to trust in his parents' unconditional love. So, he understood that the safest, least confusing path was to trust in yourself alone.

He returned to sit down opposite Liyana, handed her her glass, saw the seriousness of her expression, the slight shadow in her eyes and he waited for her to speak, didn't want to rush her in any way.

'The stakes are higher than I told you. Being caught on camera in a clinch would always be bad publicity but right now it would have even more of a negative impact.' A sip of wine and then she met his gaze full on. 'Two months ago, my parents were approached by the ruler of a neighbouring kingdom. They want to make an alliance and to cement that alliance through a royal marriage. They propose that their second son, Prince Luis, should marry me.'

The words hit him like an unexpected punch to the gut. The idea of Liyana, the woman he'd just held in his arms, the woman who'd kissed him as if there were no tomorrow, could be thinking about marrying someone else felt wrong. Whoa, Lorenzo! It had been a kiss. One kiss.

‘Have you agreed?’ He kept his voice even; this was Liyana’s life, and yet, even knowing exactly how dog in the manger he was being, he was aware of an intense desire to go and find Prince Luis and kick him round his kingdom. Very mature, Lorenzo.

‘No. But I am considering the idea.’

He chose his words carefully. ‘But you rejected the idea of an arranged marriage before. Why are you considering it now?’

‘I have no wish to marry for love again.’ Her voice absolute and definitive, holding a wealth of sadness and determination.

Of course she didn’t. Her love marriage had ended in grief and pain and loss. Who could blame her for not wanting to risk a repeat? For wanting safety, security, rules and boundaries. Wasn’t that exactly what he’d invoked himself when they had discussed Ashan’s marriage?

‘But you do want to get married again?’ he asked.

‘I think so. To help my country but also because I would like to have children. That is important to me and the only way for me to do that is through marriage.'

Another thing that had been taken away from her when her husband died. All she said made sense, put things into perspective. Whatever there was between himself and Liyana it was nothing compared to this, to her future, her life. For a moment he imagined Liyana as a mother, holding a newborn baby in her arms, and a rush of emotion surged through him, and for one brief second a hazy image of a man formed next to her, a man he recognised as himself. Now a sudden panic spiralled through him and he blinked, banished the picture from his mind.

Lorenzo had no intention of having children. He had no idea how his own upbringing would have affected him, had no idea if he could even be a good father. What if he was like either Matt or Roberto? The former had done nothing but belittle him, the latter had rejected him sight unseen. What if through nature or nurture Lorenzo turned out the same as either man? He would never risk putting any child through even a fraction of the rejection he had gone through.

'Would Prince Luis be a good father?' The question dropped from his lips without thought and he could hear the urgent undertone to his voice, could see her surprise at the question. She tucked a stray tendril of hair behind her ear as she thought.

'I don't know. But it is something we would discuss. That's the good thing about a marriage like this—you can put it all on the table at the beginning. If I have any glimmer that he wouldn't be a good father I won't marry him. I need a man who will be a good parent. A man who loves his children and wants to spend time with them. Will listen to them and put them first.'

God knew, Lorenzo agreed with every word of that.

'Believe in them,' he said. 'Love them for who they are. Be there for them and cheer them on when they take their first steps, whatever and whenever those steps are. Be there for them when things are going well and when things are tricky. Love them unconditionally.' He noticed that Liyana was looking at him with curiosity and tried a smile and a shrug. 'Something like that anyway.'

'It sounds to me as if you want children too.'

Lorenzo shook his head. 'Absolutely not.' Theory was one thing, practice another. 'It's not for me; it wouldn't suit my lifestyle. If I don't want to share my life with a partner, then how can I ever presume to think I could commit to the responsibility of a child?' But that doesn't mean I don't agree on the importance of Prince Luis being a good parent. How well *do* you know him?' Lorenzo could hear the edge in his voice, but, damn it, he felt edgy at the thought of this prince who could offer what Liyana said she wanted.

'I have met him at social functions over the years. He seems nice enough.'

'Nice enough? That's hardly enough to marry someone, is it?' Liyana's eyes narrowed, but Lorenzo didn't care if he was overstepping. The idea of Liyana marrying someone based on being 'nice enough' had tipped him over the edge. 'What about a spark, a zing, a connection?' The kiss they had shared rocked through his mind and he closed it down, knew he should be being impartial, unsure why it was such a struggle.

'Spark and zing? In case you haven't noticed, they are exactly the sort of thing that gets you into trouble.' There was snap to her voice as she jutted her chin out defiantly. 'I don't want spark or zing. No. But that doesn't matter. I am pretty sure plenty of relationships don't start with some sort of spark or zing. But most importantly spark and zing isn't what I am looking for.'

Lorenzo knew she was right. A spark of attraction was presumably what had led his mother and Roberto Rossi into infidelity. An infidelity that had led in turn to further betrayal and lies. Dominoes crashing down. Once again, the enormity of what they had done swept over him. Karen had lied to Matt, made him believe he had fathered twins, had nurtured that lie for twenty-eight years. Roberto Rossi had fathered twins and walked away from them, their presence a secret he'd taken to the grave. What sort of man had he been? Had he deeply regretted the two mistakes he'd created? Had he strayed again? Lorenzo would probably never know. The idea carved a hollow feeling in the pit of his stomach.

But it had all started with a spark. So how could he blame Liyana for choosing a marriage that didn't prioritise attraction? Yet… somehow his whole being revolted at the idea that the woman who had shared that glorious kiss with him should marry someone she felt no real physical connection with.

Liyana glared at him. 'What? You don't agree? You were the one who said an arranged marriage works, talked about rules and boundaries.'

'I know what I said. But…'

'But what?'

'Nothing.' What else could he say? Liyana was entitled to choose a marriage that was safe and secure.

'Yet I still sense a but,' she said.

He hesitated, trying to work out why he was so anti the whole idea. It wasn't as though he had a personal stake, not based on one long-ago night and a kiss. Yet as he sat here and looked at her for one insane second, he thought about what it would be like to be married to Liyana, to sit like this talking, sharing ideas, to go food shopping together, to allow attraction free rein. More foolish delusions. He didn't tick a single one of her boxes, had nothing to offer. Except an attraction that was a conduit to scandal and misery. He'd seen how stricken she'd looked when she'd weighed up the potential consequences of their kiss.

This wasn't about him; he had no right to question her decisions, no stake, no skin in the game.

Yet… 'I guess I am wondering if it is all so perfect, then why haven't you started the process in the past two months? If you do have doubts, please promise me you will consider them carefully. Think about yourself as well as your country or even your desire to be a parent. Your happiness is important too.'

He knew his words had impacted, saw a shadow cross her eyes and he almost wished the words unsaid. Because they must have evoked memories; Liyana had experienced real happiness with Gregor—perhaps her doubts stemmed from settling for what surely might seem like second best.

'I promise,' she said. 'And thank you. Thank you for listening.' She rose to her feet. 'And now I really must go. It's late and although I am pretty sure everyone thinks we are with Ashan, at some point someone will work out we aren't. And Ashan told us he wasn't coming back over an hour ago.'

He rose as well, her words a further reminder of how much Liyana had to consider social etiquette and customs and how very restrictive they were. He realised too that they hadn't discussed his investment ideas.

'I understand. But there is something else I wanted to talk about. Is it possible for us to meet for dinner tomorrow? Perhaps you could show me a good venue for Ashan's stag night and we could talk at the same time?'

A slight hesitation and then she nodded. ‘Sure. I know the perfect place. I’ll message you the details and we could meet at eight tomorrow?’

‘I appreciate that.’

They walked to the door and she turned, reached up and touched his cheek, then stood on tiptoe and dropped the lightest and quickest of butterfly kisses on his cheek. ‘Truly thank you for listening and for thinking about me as a person. Not just a princess.’

There was the honk of a horn from outside and with that she was gone. Lorenzo lifted his hand to his cheek, aware that somehow that simple kiss had left a heat that he couldn’t define and needed to forget. Because he did understand the stakes now, knew there could be nothing between himself and Liyana. Not even another kiss.

CHAPTER SEVEN

LIYANA SAT AT her desk, stared at the computer screen, and tried to concentrate on the proposal she had put together. All she had to do now was proofread it for the second time and then hand it to the minister. Who would then no doubt sign it and take the credit for it.

It didn't matter, Liyana told herself. The important thing was that it was a good proposal that would hopefully help fund a workshop to produce goods that could be sold at the marketplace. A new marketplace that Liyana was trying to make a reality. Forcing herself to concentrate, she finished reading and hit the send button. Then allowed herself to think about the man she was going to meet for dinner.

She lifted a hand to her lips. Would swear they were still tingling; not only from the utter gloriousness of their lip lock, but also from that oh-so brief sense of intimacy as she'd said goodbye. But it hadn't been only the physical closeness—there had been a sense of personal closeness. She couldn't recall the last time she'd had a conversation with someone who was considering her feelings as a *person*, not just as a princess. Yesterday Lorenzo had told her to remember the woman she'd once been, later he'd told her to consider her happiness. But how could she explain to him that it wasn't so easy?

Because the woman she'd once been had made foolish decisions. That younger Liyana who had believed in love had sacrificed her duty, set aside the good of her country in pursuit of her own happiness, in pursuit of love. Only to see that love eroded and tainted, worn away by the infidelities of her husband.

How could she explain that the doubts she harboured were because she was terrified she'd judge wrongly again? Would be exchanging the freedom bought by tragedy for another marriage trap. But it was worse than that. Their kiss yesterday, a kiss that had haunted her thoughts all day, that kiss had lodged additional doubts in her mind. It was easy to airily talk of attraction being unimportant, but when she'd kissed Lorenzo, it had been all-important. And that terrified her too. That she was still capable of doing something so impulsive and foolhardy. Because if their phones hadn't interrupted them, she wasn't sure she would have stopped at a kiss.

Liyana pushed her chair back. It was time to get ready for dinner. For a dinner she probably shouldn't have agreed to. But he'd asked to discuss something. An irrational hope surged—what if he wanted to try to stop her from marrying Prince Luis? The idea was ludicrous. Why would he do that? It wasn't as though Lorenzo wanted a relationship. He had no wish for commitment, marriage or children.

Yet… The memory of the kiss, the feel of his lips against hers, the press of his body against hers persisted. Made her both angry with herself but also full of a strange, yearning joy.

The feelings persisted once back in her own home, a palatial cottage in the grounds of the palace, persisted as she tried to decide what to wear. Rummaged through her wardrobe, tried to tell herself that she should call and cancel the dinner. Knew that she wouldn't.

There could be no harm in it. They would be in a restaurant. In public.

Perhaps she was flirting with danger, but she didn't care. Searched her wardrobe again and found an outfit she had never worn, a recent gift from an up-and-coming local designer. If for once she chose to wear something a *little* less sedate, a *little* less drab and boring, so be it. So she pulled on the grey tunic with a floral motif; the embroidered light pink flowers covered the front panel of the tunic and bordered the ends of the sleeves in a gentle display of colour. The matching grey trousers plain except for a border of pink flowers at the bottom. She carefully arranged the chiffon dupatta, the long gauzy scarf, so it trailed artfully over one shoulder, the folds fluttering towards the ground.

She looked at her reflection and frowned, aware that something was wrong. No, not wrong; she looked… She couldn't put a finger on how, but she looked different. It must be the new outfit, but she knew that didn't make sense. Maybe it was the hairstyle; she wasn't wearing her long dark hair loose—hadn't done that since Gregor's death. But she'd opted for a softer style than usual, pulled up in a jewelled clip with a few stray tendrils cascading down to frame her face. Her hand hovered over her hairbrush but then a horn beeped from outside and she told herself there was no chance to change styles now. This was it. For better or worse. It wouldn't be *decorous* to be late.

Liyana arrived at the restaurant and smiled at the staff member who recognised her from previous dinners, usually with Ashan and occasionally with friends, though in truth her friendships were more surface friendships simply because of the sheer exhaustion of having to maintain the façade that Gregor had been a wonderful man and her marriage an idyll.

'Mr Cavendish is already here,' the manager explained. 'I will take you to the table we prepared. Mr Cavendish explained you had recommended this as a potential venue for a dinner he would like to have with His Royal Highness so I have given you the table I would give them. Secluded enough for privacy and security, but close enough that you can enjoy the music and the ambiance.'

'Thank you, Ruvin.'

'You are welcome.' He paused. 'Mr Cavendish seems to be a very nice man.'

She followed the manager to the table, beautifully set, ornately carved candle holders down the middle casting a flickering light over the deep mahogany top, highlighting the beautiful setting. And despite all her best intentions her heart gave a hop and a skip as Lorenzo rose to his feet. He looked drop-dead gorgeous and it took all her effort to keep her 'perfect princess' smile in place.

'This is beautiful, Ruvin.'

'And for Prince Ashan we would add a few more personal touches. Perhaps something about the English football team he supports and of course his love of cricket.'

'How well you know us.'

Before she could say anything else there was an excited shout of 'Princess Liyana' and a small girl with long black hair braided into two plaits came racing in, past Ruvin who made an attempt to stop her.

'Mia, sweetheart. I told you not to come in. The Princess is with a guest. I apologise, Your Highness.'

'There is no need.'

'And no need to apologise on my behalf either,' Lorenzo interpolated.

'Hello, Mia.' Liyana dropped down to the little girl's level and gave her a hug, then rose, holding her hand. 'Let me introduce you to my guest,' she said. 'Lorenzo, this is Mia, Ruvin's daughter. I met her last time I was here.'

'During a refurbishment,' the manager said. 'The Princess very kindly helped to look after

Mia.' His face clouded. 'Her mother is…isn't very well at the moment…'

Mia studied Lorenzo. 'You are nearly as handsome as Prince Ashan,' she said.

Lorenzo laughed. 'Thank you very much, Mia. That is a great compliment.' He stepped forward and placed his hands together solemnly. 'It is good to meet you.'

Liyana watched as he engaged Mia in a conversation and then, 'How would you like to see some magic?' he asked.

The little girl watched wide-eyed as Lorenzo seemed to pull a sweet out of her ear and then she collapsed into giggles.

Ruvin smiled at his daughter's glee and then held out his hand. 'Come on, Mia, now we need to leave our guests to their meal.' He turned to Liyana. 'We have prepared a taster menu so Mr Cavendish can see what we have to offer. Including, of course, some of your favourite dishes.'

Once he and Mia had gone Liyana turned to Lorenzo. 'Thank you for being so kind to Mia. It's a difficult time for them. Her mother isn't well; we are hoping she is on the road to recovery but it's hard for them. I've been trying to help. I send Rosa to babysit where possible but sometimes Mia just wants to be with her dad. So it was lovely to see her laugh.' She saw Lorenzo was looking at her with curiosity. 'What's wrong?'

'Nothing. But I can see that you really care.'

'Of course I do. I know how hard Ruvin has worked and his wife as well. He co-owns this restaurant and it means the world to him. And who couldn't care for Mia? She is adorable.' Now it was her turn to look curious. 'And where did you learn magic tricks? It doesn't seem to be the sort of thing you'd learn en route to owning a global business. Or delivering pizzas, for that matter.'

She studied his expression, saw a small flush touch his face. Was he embarrassed? Was it something he didn't want to admit?

For a moment she wasn't sure whether Lorenzo would answer or not and then he shrugged. 'I volunteer,' he said. 'A few times a month at a respite centre for foster kids, or kids who have a troubled home life. It's a place where people can come and find a place to be if they have to get out of home. Its aim is to keep kids off the street or out of trouble or simply provide somewhere warm with things to do. A place that offers training and counselling and support. Anyway, a few of the kids bring in their younger siblings and I've picked up some ways to entertain them on the way. They don't get a lot of laughter in their lives, but what I find incredibly warming is, however tough their home lives are, a lot of kids still can find joy in small things.'

Liyana listened, heard the passion in his voice and, somehow, she knew that what she was about to say was true. 'You set up the respite centre, didn't you?'

He stilled. 'Yes, I did.'

Liyana looked at him, wondered now if he'd had a troubled childhood himself, knew it wasn't a question she could ask. So instead, she said, 'I think that is a wonderful thing to have done and, if you don't mind, I'd like to pick your brains on how it works. As I told you, there is a lot of poverty here still and a lot of teenagers are unemployed and that is leading to an increase in crime in some areas. I'd love to help stop that.'

'And I'd love to help.' He sipped his drink, sampled some of the food. 'In fact, that is sort of what I wanted to discuss with you.'

'A respite centre?'

'No. Let me explain. I am currently looking to diversify. I will always be part of and committed to Take It Away but now it is established I want to also do other things. Invest in different projects. Everything you have told me about Carathi, your ideas, looking around—the potential is immense; I'd love to invest here. Help your plans to encourage small businesses, invest in building a hotel.' He tapped his fingers on the table. 'We could even tie it in with the teenage unemployment. Offer employment to those who need it. Offer jobs to some of those young adults, older teens. Making sure wages are fair and conditions are good. Anyway, what do you think?'

'I think… I think it is an amazing idea, all of it. Any of it.' A sense of elation filled Liyana along with a warmth engendered by the knowledge that she'd inspired Lorenzo to want to invest in her country. 'I'll get a meeting set up for you to meet the minister. My parents may want to be involved as well. Perhaps not at any initial meeting but after that.'

There was a pause. 'What about you?' he asked.

Liyana shook her head. 'I told you. I am not a frontperson or a person with any real responsibility.'

Lorenzo shook his head. 'I promise I listened to what you said about wanting or being happy to be in the background. But I would like you to consider being part of this. Your ideas made me want to invest; I can't see the point of not involving you directly.' He met her gaze. 'What happened last night, our attraction, has nothing to do with this investment. I want you to be involved because I trust you to run the projects.'

A buzz ran through her; the idea of being actively involved from start to finish, of being given responsibility, of being part of this filled her with a sense of purpose and happiness. Intensified by the idea that he believed in her in a way even her parents didn't. 'Thank you. I won't let you down.'

'I know that. I know you want what is best for Carathi but I also know you will share my ethos. To make sure workers are paid fairly, that working conditions are of the highest standard. So I need you at the table. Present at all the meetings. I'm here for another few weeks so we should be able to get things in place. What do you think?'

'I think I am blown away—I would love to be part of this and you truly can trust me.' A small voice at the back of her mind realised what this meant: continued, legitimate contact over the next weeks, continued legitimate contact even when Lorenzo had left. Professional contact, she reminded herself. This was for her country and she wouldn't jeopardise that in any way and yet anticipation bubbled inside her.

He raised his glass. 'To our partnership.'

Liyana clinked her glass against his and smiled. 'Now let's brainstorm,' she said just as the waiter arrived with the array of food.

And as they ate and talked, discussed possible projects and plans, arranged to meet the following day so she could show him a potential venue to build a hotel, a place that would also be possible for the wedding ceremony, Liyana realised that time was literally flying, that something strange and new was happening. Oh, the attraction was still there, simmering under the surface, but it felt as though the air sparked with a whole new connection forming. And as she studied him, saw the passion in his eyes as he spoke about what he wanted to do, saw the commitment as the shadows and light illuminated his face, saw the strength of his hand, curled around his wine glass, the strong column of his throat, she felt a frisson of desire shudder through her. Desire and a sense of connection. The ideas they were discussing mattered to them both; they shared the same principles and goals. The knowledge deepened the attraction and she was powerless to stop it. All she wanted to do now was reach out, touch the muscular forearm, touch the strong jawline, feel the six o'clock stubble under her fingers. She wanted this evening to never end.

She knew it had to. Yet she was trying to make the final morsel of food last and it was only the sound of Ruvin's throat clearing that snapped her from the spell.

'I was wondering if when you have dined with Ashan you would wish to go on somewhere else. If so you could maybe check out a nearby bar where they play live music. It is just round the corner.'

'What do you think?' Lorenzo said. 'It sounds like it could be fun.'

Fun. The word a sudden reminder of their night seven years ago. A small voice in the back of her head bleeped 'danger' and she resolutely shut it down. This wasn't seven years ago. There was no possibility of their evening ending up as it had all those years before.

'It sounds like a good idea to see if it would work,' Liyana said, hoping she sounded suitably calm.

Yet as they walked, protected by cover of the darkness, she allowed herself to walk a little closer than perhaps was wise to his bulk, the strength of his body, felt her own body almost unfurl as it was trying to get closer and closer still.

Until they reached the venue Ruvin had mentioned.

As they entered the dimly illuminated basement, Liyana heard the traditional sound of drums, and the music sent a surge of adrenalin through her. She looked round at the brick walls covered in memorabilia, the curve of the bar in the corner, the tables arranged around the edge of a dance floor where the band were in full swing.

They edged through the crowd, who were completely oblivious to the presence of royalty, and found a table in the corner.

'Drink?' Lorenzo asked.

'A pineapple juice, please,' Liyana requested. She had no intention of adding any further buzz to her already buzzing body and brain. Because all she wanted, all she craved was to be Elina Perera again. For a night. She wanted to dance, let her hair down. She wanted to dance with Lorenzo, stand close to him, press her body against his as his arms encircled her, as they swayed to the haunting rhythmic beat of the drums.

But she knew she couldn't.

Knew she mustn't.

Had to restrain the impulse that could undo all the good they had done today. Closing her eyes, she tried to centre herself, remind herself that she was a princess, remind herself what was at stake.

He came back, holding two drinks, followed by a group of people.

'You've been rumbled,' he said. 'The bartender saw us come in and recognised you.'

Instinctively Liyana bade her demeanour to become that of a decorous princess, and soon they were engaged in conversation with the three young people, who turned out to be students. A few minutes later they were joined by others, all of them interested in speaking with their princess. Until one woman glanced at her watch and then turned to look from Liyana to Lorenzo.

'I am one of the troupe of dancers about to perform. Would you both like to participate in the traditional dance?'

Liyana glanced at Lorenzo, who smiled. 'I'd love to. I may not be a natural but I'd love to try.'

It wasn't exactly what Liyana had wanted but as they headed to the dance floor, encouraged by the other dancers to join in, as they heard the notes of the traditional Cathari folk song, the words speaking of long-ago lovers parted and brought together again by the intervention of the gods, as they followed the moves, the world seemed to take on a different hue.

There was laughter as Lorenzo was shown the moves and then something seemed to click and despite the other people on the dance floor, despite the noise and the chatter, it seemed as if there were only the two of them. So near and yet so far, just like the imprisoned lovers of the song. Both of them caught in the words in a shimmering net of awareness, their bodies mirroring each other but unable to touch, and she was aware of gnawing yearning in the pit of her tummy, fuelled by the sheer craving of a raw, visceral, aching desire.

Until the music ended and she somehow pulled herself back to the real world, took a smiling bow as their audience clapped as they returned to their table. *Princess Perfect.* For a brief minute they sat in slightly shell-shocked silence; it took all her willpower not to reach out to at least take some succour from a brief touch, a fleeting brush of their hands. But before she could think of anything to say, more people came to join them, carrying more drinks, and she welcomed the need to put the princess mask back on.

As the evening progressed, she admired Lorenzo's ability to speak and chat when she knew his longing matched hers, and so she smiled and conversed even as desire continued to thrum and fizz inside her. *Princess Perfect.* A desire she knew to be impossible, unwanted but threatening to consume her. A desire that continued to strum through her long after she had returned home to sleep alone. *Princess Perfect.*

CHAPTER EIGHT

THE FOLLOWING MORNING, Lorenzo stood at the dock, saw Liyana climb out of the car and head towards him and his breath caught in his throat. She was wearing a dress rather than her favoured salwar kameez, a long-sleeved white dress that floated down to her ankles, her hair pulled back in a ponytail under a ribboned straw boater hat. She looked stunning and he had to force himself to remain still, his whole body taut with sheer frustrated desire, a knock-on from the previous night and dreams laced with images of Liyana. But he waited, oh-so aware of the man who had moved forward to greet her, knew he must be the skipper of the royal boat that was going to take them to a different part of Carathi, a secluded beach area, accessible only by boat.

As they approached, Lorenzo was careful to keep his distance, even once they were alone and he could hear the chug of the motor as the boat began its journey. Somehow silence seemed like the best option, the only way to contain the simmering awareness left over from the night before. He gazed out at the azure silver-topped waves, slightly rippled by the gentlest of breezes, glinting in the rays of the overhead sun that basked down from a cloudless sky.

But despite the serene beauty of the journey, he was transported back to the night before, the sound of the drums, the dimly lit interior, the laughter and chat, the taste and tang of pineapple. And Liyana. The sinuous grace of her dancing, the sparkle of her brown eyes, and the way that somehow, despite the people, it had felt as though it were just the two of them, their bodies conducting their own private conversation, tantalising with promises that could never be fulfilled.

Masked desire, the excruciating agony of being so close to Liyana, the memory of the jasmine scent of her shampoo seemed to mix with the salt tang of the sea. His body ached with a yearning that still lingered now in the ocean-fresh air, surrounded by sparkling water, and approaching the curving edge of golden-sand-strewn beaches. And as he looked across at her, saw the slight strain in her brown eyes, the way her hands clenched, the tension in her body, he knew that Liyana felt exactly the same, was holding herself back by sheer effort of will, weighted by the knowledge they must not, should not, could not risk the lightest of touches.

Because they both knew this attraction had nowhere to go. She met his gaze and he was sure her thoughts were in line with his, just as their bodies had matched each other's rhythm in the dance.

He saw her lips upturn in what he recognised as her princess smile and before he could speak, she did.

'I wanted to thank you,' she said. 'For your investment proposals. I spoke with Ashan this morning and my parents and they are all looking forward to what we come up with.' Now her smile widened, touched her eyes. 'My parents were pleased and they have agreed that I can take a place at the table as you asked. They like the idea of the hotel.'

Lorenzo nodded, reminded himself that this was how their relationship had to be—a professional one; he was utterly serious about investment in Carathi. Over the past days with Liyana he had felt a surprising connection to the kingdom, could see its potential exactly as Liyana could.

He believed the investment itself to be sound but it was also a way to support Ashan and the country he would one day rule. Ashan, who was another reason why he knew all thoughts of attraction must be shelved. As a ruler Ashan would want Liyana to marry Prince Luis; certainly, he would prefer that marriage to a clandestine affair with Lorenzo. Come to that, he would prefer marriage to a prince to marriage with Lorenzo. Ashan believed royalty should marry royalty.

'I'm looking forward to exploring the area.'

The boat gently bumped as it docked and after thanking the captain and arranging to be picked up in the late afternoon they disembarked.

'I thought we'd walk for a while so you can see the landscape, including the royal banyan tree, because it was said to be planted by one of my ancestors centuries ago. Then we can catch a tuk tuk to one of the most secluded beaches. A possible resort location. Then we can do a tour looking for suitable properties to use for the wedding ceremony.'

'Sounds like a plan.'

As they walked, their strides somehow completely attuned, he was still so very aware of Liyana. The way her ponytail swung as she walked, the crinkle of her forehead when she thought, the graceful movement of her hands in the sun-warmed air as she made a point or gestured to something she wished him to see.

And when they stopped at the ancient banyan tree and she told stories of how she and Ashan had played there, made up tales of pirates and knights, her smile lit her face and he could imagine the young Liyana revelling in being the princess of her imagination rather than the one restricted by rules and regulations.

Here, where they saw few people, none of whom showed any interest in them, he could almost imagine they were two normal people, tourists perhaps, a couple, and he felt his palms itch with a desire to reach out and take her hand. Wished that just for a day they could be a couple.

But even as he thought that, a real couple, clearly tourists, approached. 'Excuse me? You're Gregor Mertens' wife, aren't you? Oh my God. I can't believe it. Could we have a photo?'

He felt Liyana freeze beside him, and then she smiled. It wasn't her princess smile, but it was a practised one. It didn't crinkle her eyes in the same way her real smile did and he sensed tension in her body, though her tone was polite, welcoming even. 'Yes, I am and of course you can.'

'I am so sorry that you lost him,' the tourist continued. 'He was the most amazing man.'

'We are his number one fans. The way he raced, the risks he pulled off…the man was a marvel and such a loss,' the man chipped in.

'You must still be devastated. Your romance was so beautiful, such a fairy story. He must have been such a wonderful husband.'

Lorenzo had stepped back by now, but he could sense Liyana's discomfort. And it wasn't surprising; however well meaning these tourists were, they must be bringing back memories. Of her fairy-tale marriage.

Yet she widened the fake smile. 'Thank you. I know how much all his fans meant to Gregor, each and every one of you. I know he would be touched by everything you have said. Thank you for your sympathy.' Lorenzo watched as she posed for a photograph, waited until the couple had left before stepping forward, hoping he could somehow dispel the memories that must have been evoked for Liyana.

'Are you OK?' he asked.

'I'm fine,' she said, the words belied by the tightness in her voice, the rigidity in her shoulders.

'Sorry. That was a pointless question. You don't have to pretend to be fine. Meeting people like that must hurt, must bring it all back.'

'Yes. It does. But I *am* fine.'

Lorenzo remained silent as they walked, followed Liyana to a place where within minutes a tuk tuk came to a stop. They climbed in and, looking at her shuttered expression, he found it hard to equate this Liyana with the one from earlier. It was as though she'd closed in on herself.

They reached the beach, thanked the driver and she led the way across a stretching curve of golden beach, deserted sand as far as the eye could see, lapped by the roll of silver-topped waves and dotted with palm trees, green fronds waving lazily in the breeze. As they walked, they both slipped their shoes off and the sun-warmed grains scrunched under his feet, Liyana almost marching.

'Liyana?' She turned to him and he could see so much emotion in her face it twisted his heart. 'Why don't we stop for a bit?' he suggested. 'It's OK to be sad, to grieve, to be silent with your thoughts and memories.' He looked out at the vast expanse of sea. 'Why don't we sit down for a while?'

She hesitated, then sat down on the sand, hugged her knees and looked out at the rolling waves, the breeze blowing the tendrils of hair around her face.

Liyana stared out at the sea, registered that the waves were choppier, a roil of dark blue now, and she felt as though somehow the sea were mirroring her mood. The encounter with the tourists had shaken her, way more than it normally would. Usually, she simply played her part on automatic; she would never do anything to sully Gregor's image, or ruin his fans' devotion to him.

But today playing that part in front of Lorenzo made her uncomfortable. Worse than uncomfortable: she felt…mixed up, angry… It felt wrong to see and hear *his* sympathy. The tourists didn't matter. Gregor *had* been a Formula One champion, he had been a brilliant driver, a man who took life-or-death risks in the pursuit of glory on the track. Liyana knew the least she owed Gregor's memory was to play the part of devoted wife. It was a way to alleviate at least a little of the guilt she felt. But for the first time in years, she wanted to tell the truth, wanted Lorenzo to know the real Liyana, because in just days he had somehow got under her skin, seen past the princess persona. To the real woman underneath.

But did she *really* want Lorenzo to know about her marriage, the horrible truth of it, the fact she had made such a monumental mistake, that in fact her pursuit of love had been an abject failure, that she'd been belittled and humiliated and betrayed? Did she actually want him to know the real ugly truth about her, that she could feel even a glimmer of silver lining in a tragic death? That took selfishness to soaring heights—could she expose her real self to Lorenzo, see the connection they'd formed fizzle away? Because that connection was based on his belief that Liyana was a grieving widow. He'd offered her compassion and sympathy and she had repaid it with more lies.

Better to let him believe the lie. Or was it?

But before she could say anything, do anything, even crystallise what she wanted to do, a flash of lightning streaked across the sky, followed by a low boom of thunder.

And she realised that she'd been so inwardly focused that she'd missed any signs of the incoming storm, just as large droplets of rain began to fall from a suddenly stormy sky, the previously blue sky scudded now with grey clouds that swirled ominously as the wind picked up speed, skimming and shifting the golden grains of sand.

They scrambled to their feet and Lorenzo took her hand in his and even now, when she knew a tropical storm was brewing, when she knew the intensity and damage the storms could do, even now a jolt went through her. They scanned the deserted beach, squinting through the whirls and whorls of sand.

'I think I saw a hut before,' she shouted, the wind carrying and distorting the words, and she tugged him in the right direction.

They half walked, half ran, now buffeted by the wind and half blinded by the sand as the rain began to fall in earnest as she tried to locate the hut, finally seeing the outline of the building. They raced towards it, breathed a sigh of relief when the door pushed open. It was sparsely furnished, a table and a couple of chairs and a braided mat on the floor, some fishing nets in a corner.

'It must be a fisherman's hut. We're lucky we found it,' he said. 'Hopefully it's weathered many a storm. I guess we will have to stay here until it stops.'

Liyana listened to the wind howling outside;

ever since Gregor's death storms had unsettled her, caused swirls of foreboding, heightened anxiety at the thought of the damage they could wreak, the way nature could impose senseless tragedy. Without thinking she moved closer to Lorenzo's reassuring strength and bulk.

Jumped when the door to the hut swung open with a thud, spun round to see a soaked man, drenched despite the waterproof clothing he wore. A man who managed a smile through the droplets of rain on his face.

'I'm from the storm-patrol team. Someone told me they saw a pair of tourists dropped off at the beach a couple of hours back. Come on. The storm is due to last overnight. I'll get the two of you to safety.'

Liyana realised the man hadn't recognised her; hardly surprising given she was drenched and right now the man had more to think or worry about than identifying royalty. And she and Lorenzo had been standing close enough that there was clearly an assumption they were a tourist couple. And she'd rather it stayed that way if possible. The rescue committee had enough to do without worrying about protocol.

'Thank you,' she said.

'OK. Let's go. It's due to get worse. We need to hurry.'

They followed the man out into the gale, and just for a second Liyana hesitated before getting into the car, a sudden unbidden vision of Gregor's final moments at the wheel of a car in a storm assailing her. Pushing them down and exhorting herself not to hold up this good man who had come to rescue them at peril to himself, she clambered in, but as the car lurched its way through the driving rain, buffeted by the wind, she could feel trepidation rise and surge, welcomed, took courage from, the steadying clasp of Lorenzo's hand around hers.

The car pulled to a stop and the driver turned to them. 'I've got other people to locate,' he said. 'So I'm going to have to drop you off at the guest house my wife and I run. We have empty rooms and we are happy to provide shelter.'

'Thank you.'

'And good luck,' Lorenzo said. 'We truly appreciate your courage.'

Liyana translated quickly and they climbed out of the car, ran through the downpour to the front door of the bungalow, and entered.

The woman at the desk smiled, though her

smile looked distracted and Liyana guessed she was worried about her husband. Felt her own stomach twist in sympathy. 'We have one room left, which you are welcome to have. I have put towels in each room.' She glanced quickly at Liyana, who stepped slightly backwards, relieved that the room was dark and shadowy.

'Thank you.'

Lorenzo stepped forward shielding Liyana from view as much as he could. 'This is very kind of you and it is brave of your husband to do the job he does.'

'It is the least we can do. Our country has a history of kindness to strangers. I have put some food in the rooms as well.' She handed Lorenzo a key. 'I am not sure how long the storm will last but you are welcome to stay overnight or until the storm finishes.'

A few minutes later Liyana and Lorenzo were inside the guest room, which was clean and simply furnished. A double bed against one wall, two bedside cabinets, a white wooden wardrobe and a small table by the window, everything gleaming. Liyana turned to look at him.

'Thank you for not saying who I am. It would make things complicated and I didn't want to delay the rescue patrol in any way. My identity is irrelevant when there are people out there risking their lives.'

'Will your parents send out a search party?' he asked.

'They can't.' She pulled her phone from her pocket, checked. 'Too dangerous in the storm and they have no way of contacting me. Power is down.' She also guessed they wouldn't want to broadcast that they were stranded in a storm together unchaperoned. 'There really is nothing they can do.'

She walked over to the window, heard her voice catch, couldn't help but think now of Gregor and those fateful last seconds when he'd wrenched the wheel, made one fatal miscalculation that storm-buffeted night.

Heard Lorenzo mutter under his breath and then sensed him behind her, the sheer masculine, reassuring bulk of him.

'I'm sorry,' he said softly. 'I know Gregor's accident happened in a storm. Come on, come away from the window. I'll light the candles and we can eat something.'

Liyana turned, watched as he laid out the flatbreads alongside small bowls of aubergine salad and a variety of fruit. Pride touched her that her people were so kind, had an ethos where community meant helping each other and strangers.

'You should eat,' he said softly. 'Even if it's just a distraction.' He waited as she helped herself and then followed suit and Liyana welcomed the familiar taste and tang of cumin, the slight bitterness of the aubergine complemented by the spices, and the texture of the bread.

Once they'd eaten, he hesitated. 'Would it help to talk? Talk about the accident? Or talk and remember Gregor? Or is that too painful?' He gave a small smile. 'If you prefer to sit in silence, I'm good with that too. Whatever helps.'

Liyana looked across at him, the same emotions churning inside her from earlier, guilt over Gregor's death, guilt that she was deceiving this caring man. There was nothing but concern in Lorenzo's blue eyes and as the rain beat at the window panes and she heard the rattling howl of the wind she knew she could not sit here and accept sympathy and compassion for a lie. Compassion she didn't even deserve. She knew with bone-deep certainty that she could trust this man. Moreover right here, right now, she wanted him to know the truth.

She knew there could be no future for them.

She wanted children, wanted to make a marriage that was good for her country, do her duty. Prove to herself that she could be a princess worthy of Carathi. Lorenzo had no wish for children or marriage or any form of commitment. Their lives could only ever touch tangentially.

But that wasn't what was at stake here. Here in this hotel room, where no one knew who they were, with a storm raging outside, where men and women werc putting their lives on the line, she refused to hide behind a lie. For a brief period of time, she wanted to lay down the princess mask, wanted Lorenzo to know who the real Liyana was.

'I would like to talk,' she said, giving a ghost of a smile. 'I want you to know the truth. I'm not… It's not how everyone thinks.'

CHAPTER NINE

LORENZO KNEW THAT what Liyana was about to share was something deeply personal, something that it wouldn't be easy to confide. His heart twisted in his chest as he saw the pain in her eyes, the lines of strain etched on her face. Reaching out, he touched her hand gently.

'You don't have to tell me anything if you don't want to. I know it must be hard to remember what you've lost.' He could see how haunted her eyes looked, had sensed her fear, her trepidation, in the car as she'd clung onto his hand. 'And I know how difficult it must be, holding it together, and you've done incredibly, to manage your grief and still achieve so much and present such a serene face to the world. I just wanted you to know you don't have to do that with me. You can say what you want.'

She made a sudden noise, one of dissent. 'I'm not the person everyone believes me to be.' The words sounded taut, stretched tight as she met his gaze. Carefully he pushed the empty food containers to one side, reached out and took her hand in his, wanted her to know that whatever she had to say he would listen, was there.

'Gregor's death was on a night like this. Though it wasn't a freak storm like this one; it was a predicted storm, but he wasn't worried. I wasn't worried—Gregor *enjoyed* driving in difficult conditions. Somehow the way he was…it didn't occur to anyone that he would make a mistake. Perhaps he didn't. Perhaps it wasn't possible to drive that particular road at that particular time however skilled you were.' She shook her head.

'The press analysed it endlessly but in the end it didn't matter. The tragedy couldn't be undone by rehashing it. His car went over the cliff and he died. At first it was all such a blur, the shock, I somehow couldn't believe it, because Gregor was so vital, so full of life. Then the grief. Because I did grieve.' Her voice was oddly defiant. And then she took a deep breath. 'I'm not sure when I realised what his death meant.' Her voice was small now. 'It freed me.'

Lorenzo frowned as he tried to process the words, instinctively tightened his grip on her hand as she tried to pull it away. 'I'm not sure I understand,' he said, though as he looked at her face, saw the emotions chase their way across, shadows of sadness and guilt, he began to suspect.

'My marriage to Gregor. It…it wasn't the fairy tale that everyone believes.' She gave a small laugh. 'It was at first, or at least I thought it was.' She looked away, towards the window where the rain still beat in a relentless driving onslaught.

'I met Gregor when I was twenty-two on a state visit to Italy with Ashan. I was beginning to go out in public and I was enjoying the new duties, enjoying seeing new places, meeting new people. But I was also so very conscious of everything I wasn't allowed to do, how chaperoned and protected I still was, especially compared to the people I was meeting. So when Gregor asked if he could meet me on my own for a coffee I decided to rebel, to meet him. This was Gregor Mertens, after all; I couldn't believe he'd be interested in me.

'So I managed to sneak away and that's how it all started. I was swept off my feet by the sheer romance of it—he was the man every woman wanted and he'd fallen for *me*. He pulled out all the stops, my head was awhirl with the glamour, the romance and…and then he proposed—a romantic, extravagant, public proposal of love. Instead of a negotiated alliance, a man who I believed wanted to marry me for myself. And on top of that a whole new world without rules and restrictions.

'I was giddy, intoxicated, in love and I said yes… My parents weren't happy because they were blindsided, but they had no real choice but to accept it because the press had already gone wild. I knew they were disappointed but I told myself it would be OK, that I could still be a good princess, that Gregor had fame and wealth and he would be a good ambassador for Carathi. That once they saw how happy we were they would be happy for me. Excuse after excuse.'

He heard the bitterness in her voice.

'They weren't excuses, they were valid points. You couldn't walk away from love, sacrifice your happiness and his.'

'Only it wasn't like that,' she said, and now the bitter note was laced with sadness.

'What happened?'

'It took me a few months to realise that I'd made a mistake, that the romance was an illusion, the love a stage prop not a reality. That I'd swapped one set of rules for another. Gregor *hadn't* wanted me, he'd wanted a princess, to marry royalty. I was like a trophy to him, something he'd won and could show off. And once he'd won me, he was ready to put me on a shelf, keep me, but move on to the next conquest, the next trophy.

'About six months after we got married, I found out Gregor wasn't keen on fidelity. Or at least his. He thought that he was different from everyone else. Entitled to do whatever he wanted. He saw being with him as a competition with him the prize. He expected me to be grateful that I'd won the wedding ring, but to accept that I'd have to compete with other women, to fight for him. Like it was a game or a race.'

'With a whole different set of rules,' he said quietly.

'Yes. The first time I couldn't quite believe it. That he'd been unfaithful. The shock, the hurt, the humiliation.' He could hear all the emotion in her voice and he swallowed down an anger against Gregor so strong he could hardly breathe.

'Why didn't you leave?' He kept all judgement from his voice; after all, his mother hadn't left Matt.

Her hand tightened round his. 'At first all

I could think of was the scandal. How much more disappointed my parents would be if the press got hold of the story. All I wanted was for it to remain a secret. I told myself that perhaps it wouldn't happen again. That I needed to work at the marriage. I couldn't believe I'd got it so wrong, that what I had thought was an idyll was an illusion, a fake.'

'But it did happen again?'

'Yes. And the worst of it was Gregor didn't care. He'd already made it plain that he had no interest in Carathi. Told me his infidelity was my fault; that we didn't need to work at our marriage. *I* did. That it was my fault he was forced to look elsewhere. And my problem if it bothered me. That he risked his life every time he went on the track so he had no intention of wasting his life. If he wanted to sleep with someone else, he would. The only way to stop it was to try harder, compete better. It made me feel like a failure on all fronts, as though I wasn't good enough.'

Again, just as she had never felt she was a good enough princess, then she'd felt she wasn't a good enough wife. His chest ached as he saw the slight droop of her shoulders as she looked back to the past.

'So I tried harder, for the next two and a half

years, I entered the race. I did compete. I tried to wear the right clothes, look the part, be the part. Be an adoring wife. I almost believed that his fame, his fortune, his job meant he should be allowed his infidelities, if I wasn't good enough to hold him. I was desperate to prove I could be the perfect wife. That I hadn't failed in another role.'

Lorenzo shook his head. 'No. Don't. It wasn't you, Liyana. This was on him. Everything you have told me about him makes me want to shake him, tell him to appreciate what he had. A beautiful, caring, vital woman.' But he could see that she didn't believe him. 'It's the truth,' he said quietly.

'I tried so hard…

'To please him, to be the person he wanted you to be?'

Liyana stilled. 'Yes. That's it exactly.' She stared at him. 'How do you know?'

Lorenzo turned to face her, wanted to answer her question, to share his own experience to see if it would help her, if it could do anything to give comfort, to show solidarity and empathy.

'Because I did the same, not to a wife or partner, but to my…' he hesitated '…to my father.' There was no need to muddy the water just yet with the full story. 'That's how I know how it feels.'

Now it was Liyana's turn to frown in perplexion. 'Tell me,' she said.

Liyana looked at him, could hear from his voice, his tone, that Lorenzo really did get it even if she wasn't sure why, and she wanted to know why, wanted to listen to his story, to understand him better, to offer comfort and support as he was to her. After a moment he began.

'Growing up it was really clear that my father...well, he quite simply didn't like me.' His voice was matter-of-fact but she could hear the embedded pain. 'It's something I *always* knew. He'd come home from work and I'd run over to him to tell him something and he'd ignore me, or say something negative that made me feel small or stupid. However hard I tried. I'd draw pictures to the "best dad", I'd do projects on his football team.' There was self-mockery in his voice now. 'I tried to look like him, dress like him. But everything I did was wrong. Not good enough. He'd put down every idea I had, criticise everything I did, tell me I'd amount to nothing.'

Liyana didn't know what to say, couldn't

imagine how anyone could do that to any child, let alone his own, the sheer cruelty of it chilling. In the end she said, 'You must know that it wasn't you. How could it be?'

'But it wasn't him,' Lorenzo said, a weight of sadness in his voice. 'He was a great dad to my sister, my twin sister. He supported Daisy, was kind to her, helped her with her homework, he even took her to football matches. He was a good dad to her.'

'That must have been difficult for you both.'

'It was. It is. I love my sister; I really do, but I know how conflicting it was for her and for my mother. Their marriage…it's all on his terms. As long as she does as he wants it's all fine, but if she steps out of line, his line, he puts her down, bullies her. And so of course she does as he wants and then everything is "happy" again.'

'Did she stand up for you?' Liyana managed to keep her voice even, didn't feel it was right for her to judge his mother.

'In the beginning I think she did, but it didn't help. My mum, she is a very gentle person and she had no idea *how* to stand up to him. And when she tried it made things worse for her and for Daisy. And for me. So somehow over time the lines blurred and I think she started to think it was my fault in some way, because things were so much easier when I wasn't there. Plus, my father's dislike for me was so profound, so deep it was insurmountable. She never mistreated me, but she encouraged me to make myself scarce, to stay out of the way.'

He shrugged. 'I remember staying out as late as I could one day after school and coming home and I saw them, the three of them, sitting round the table laughing, playing a board game. And when I came in everything changed. My dad stopped the game, became ratty, shouted at me, shouted at my mum. Daisy ran around trying to make peace; she has always hated confrontation. And I *knew* then that I was the problem. That they were happier without me. After that I made sure I kept out of the way.'

'Where did you go?'

'Whenever I could I'd stay at school as long as possible; it was easier in summer, but I'd hang round parks, wander round the shopping mall, the library was good as well. But it was difficult.'

'That's why you set up the foundation centre.' It made so much sense and she loved the fact that Lorenzo had done something for other kids in the same boat he had once been in. Was trying to make a difference.

He nodded. 'I wanted kids to have somewhere to go. It is so easy to get in with the wrong crowd, to get into trouble, if you haven't a home to go to.'

Liyana looked at him. 'But you made good,' she said.

'Yes. Because at some point I figured out that nothing was going to change how he felt about me. He was never going to love me. Or even like me. I took all the hurt and the confusion and I channelled it into a desire to prove him wrong. Show him that I could be a success, that I wasn't the joke, the failure, the nothing that he thought I was. I wanted to prove him wrong and I wanted to give my mother a choice. An escape route. I couldn't understand why she stayed with him, but I thought maybe if I could provide her with security, a home, money, it would give her the courage, the means to leave.'

Liyana felt a swell of admiration; he'd taken something bad and managed to work out a way to make it something good. Now she understood his drive, his desire to succeed. Was touched too at his ability to not blame his mother, to not resent his sister.

'Your mum is lucky,' she said softly. 'That you cared. Did she leave?' she asked.

He shook his head. 'A couple of years ago I offered her the escape route and she refused. She said she loved Matt and she said she owed him her loyalty. I didn't know what she meant at the time but now I do.' He took a deep breath, clenched and unclenched his hands and she could see disbelief etched on his face, as he continued speaking. 'A few months ago, Daisy found some old letters; they showed that my mother had an affair before we were born. With an Italian man, Roberto Rossi, whose family owns a vineyard in Tuscany. I don't know the details of how they met or how long the affair went on for, but she fell pregnant. With Daisy and me.

'She told Roberto but he wanted nothing to do with it. He was married himself. He walked away and my mum told Matt that she was pregnant with his children.'

Liyana felt her eyes widen, her jaw drop as she tried to process the information, the fact that his mother had lived a lie for so long. The thought intruded that she was doing the same. Living a lie. And yet her lie affected only herself.

'So the man you believed to be your father,

the man who believes he is your father, isn't your birth father.'

'Yes. I contacted the man who is our birth grandfather and we had DNA testing done. It was conclusive.'

'Have you told your mother you know?'

'No. Daisy doesn't want to yet and I respect that. This is a lot harder for her. As I told you, Matt, that's our "dad", has always been good to her. The three of them are a proper family.'

'This must be hard for you *both*. Seeing your mum and knowing what you know.'

'It is hard. At first, I was furious. But the letters, they showed how desperate she was. She was terrified about facing parenthood alone, especially with twins. Her own parents had passed away when she was a child, she didn't have any family support and I suppose she must have panicked. Decided the best option was to provide us with a father and herself with security. It does explain a lot, explains why she stayed with Matt, why she felt she owed him loyalty. He did stand by her, when Roberto didn't. He agreed to marry her, Roberto walked away.'

Liyana could see that, but to her it still didn't excuse his mother standing by whilst Matt proved to not be a good father to Lorenzo.

And whilst she admired Lorenzo's ability to forgive that, it made her heart ache that Lorenzo had been made to feel it was all his fault.

'Have you met your birth family?'

'A couple of times. My birth father died when I was a child. But my grandfather is alive and I have a half-sister, Amara. She had no more idea I existed than I did her. And I'm still not sure what to do about them.'

There was a confusion in his voice, a note of bewilderment, and Liyana's heart went out to him. She tried to imagine how it must feel to be presented with a new family out of the blue.

'It is a big decision,' she said quietly, and she understood why he would have qualms. Family life wasn't something he had a good experience of—why would he want to open himself up to any more of it? Perhaps there was even a fear that his new family would reject him as Matt had, as his mother had to some degree.

'They owe me nothing,' he said. 'Roberto made it clear he didn't want us to be part of the Rossi family. I have survived twenty-eight years without them. I am not sure what the point is of meeting up.'

'Just because you don't need them doesn't mean there aren't any positives from forging some sort of bond.'

'A bond based on what? Blood? I don't believe in that. Matt couldn't love me, but you can't blame blood for that. Because he does love Daisy. Roberto loved Amara but he had no wish to even see Daisy or me, blood or no blood.'

And that had to make Lorenzo feel unwanted on so many levels, no wonder he'd rather walk alone. And in that moment Liyana was grateful for her family—there might be rules and restrictions and expectations but there was also love and affection and a bond.

Liyana thought carefully, wanted to somehow make him see that perhaps it was worth the risk, that rejection wasn't a given. Because he was a good person, worthy of love. A sudden fierce regret panged through her that she couldn't really identify and she didn't even want to try. Too scared where it would take her. Plus, this was about Lorenzo, about helping him.

'You, Daisy, your grandfather and Amara are all innocents in this. It is the actions and choices your mum and Roberto made that have impacted all of you. So maybe it is worth you all giving each other a chance. Maybe something good can come of past wrongs. I know that you are a good person and maybe your grandfather and Amara are too. And,' she said fiercely, 'they would be lucky to have you in their family.'

Lorenzo shook his head. 'I don't think it works like that. I would be intruding. Vittorio and Amara are very close; he brought her up after her parents died when she was only four. And now, now Amara is getting married to a man Vittorio clearly regards highly. They don't need me.'

'But that doesn't mean they won't benefit from knowing you.' Liyana could see from the set of his lips that Lorenzo wasn't buying it and she felt a fierce anger at his mum, at Roberto and Matt Cavendish. 'Promise me you'll think about it, think about what *you* want to do.'

He gave the smallest of smiles in acknowledgement of the fervency of her tone and nodded. 'I promise. But sometimes I wish Daisy had never found those letters. I'm sure she does too.'

'Of course you do. It must have made your head spin. That Matt isn't your father.'

'That's exactly it. My head is spinning trying to work out what it means and where it leaves me. I have spent all these years wanting to prove that I am a worthy son and I am not even his son. Spent so many years driven to succeed to prove to him that I am not a failure with no future. And now that success all feels somehow tainted, less meaningful. And my mum… She isn't the person I thought she was.'

Liyana could hear the pain in his voice, could understand how his whole life must feel skewed, viewed through a new kaleidoscope of truth.

'As for Matt, I don't even know how to think of him. He has actually been wronged all these years, been fed a lie as well. He should never have been lumbered with me in the first place.'

'No! He wasn't lumbered with you. To be given the chance to father a child is a gift that he squandered. You were a gift and it is his loss that he can't see that. I know you would have been a wonderful child. You are caring and the very fact you love your sister, that you and Daisy have a good and loving relationship, is testament to both of you. You have built up a global company and made a success of it. And that success *is* something to be proud of.'

She hesitated. 'For yourself. It doesn't matter if Matt is proud of you or not, what matters is what you have done, what you have achieved. And that comes from inside you. You are now trying to use your wealth to help others and a lot of people wouldn't do that.' More than that, he was doing it quietly. 'And you aren't just putting money in. You are giving your time. That shows true worth.'

'The same goes for you,' he said quietly. 'You have achieved so much. All that you are doing for Carathi, all that you want to do. You are trying to do good, to help people, to make people's lives better. That comes from inside you. You as a person. It is nothing to do with being a princess. That shows true worth.'

Liyana felt the all too familiar anguish wrench through her. 'No. A worthy person would never feel the way I feel about Gregor's death. I was freed; I *benefited* from his death. What sort of person does that make me if I can say that out loud, find or feel a positive to a tragedy? Gregor had his faults but he didn't deserve to die.'

'Hey, stop.' His voice was low and firm and reassuring. 'You are not saying he deserved to die or that you wished for his death. You didn't. You were trapped in a marriage made unhappy by his infidelities. You were trying to avoid scandal and you were trying to make it work. His death did free you, but what you have chosen to do with that freedom is a good thing that has benefited, is benefiting, your country.' He paused. 'As for marrying him in the first place, that wasn't wrong. You were in love. If Gregor had been a different person he could have done good for Carathi and made you happy. The fact your marriage didn't work was not your fault. It was his. And it was also his loss that he couldn't appreciate your love, couldn't see you for who you are, the caring, beautiful woman you are.'

Liyana felt tears prickle the backs of her eyelids, felt a surge of warmth, of serenity and peace, despite the sound of the storm still raging outside. A sense of a burden placed down at least temporarily and a sense of connection between herself and this man.

'Thank you. Thank you for those words and thank you for listening to me.' She looked at his face, at the oh-so familiar planes and angles, the strength of his jaw, the empathy in his deep blue eyes, the errant curl of a strand of hair, and her heart did a funny little flip. Now she couldn't help herself, wanted, needed, a physical closeness, told herself all she would do was kiss his cheek, a gesture of solidarity and appreciation. She meant only to allow herself a few precious seconds, but somehow the movement changed as her brain decided to change gears and somehow, instead of his cheek, her lips brushed against his.

The jolt, the heat, the strength of the spark shocked her, dizzied her, and she sat back and stared at him, would swear she could hear the crackle in the air as a streak of lightning flashed outside.

She told herself to stop, cease, desist. Because there could be no future. She understood now why Lorenzo didn't want love or commitment, why he'd rather trust himself to walk his path alone. But right here and now it didn't matter.

'Kaboom,' she whispered and now, gazes locked, they both rose to their feet, moved round the table, their movements so in synch and then she was entwined in his arms, and he was kissing her and she was kissing him and everything felt so gloriously right. As if this moment was fated, meant to be, his arms round her, her hands in his hair, and she revelled in the taste of him, the scent of him, the feel of him. Until finally they pulled back, their ragged breaths mingling.

Then, 'Liyana? I…' His voice husky.

Raising a hand, she touched her finger to his lips. 'It's OK. I want this. I want you. We've tried to fight it but I know if we don't do this, if I don't do this, I will regret it for ever.'

He studied her face and she knew he would see nothing but truth there. She had no reservations, no doubts—all she knew was that she wanted him. Here and now. That was all that mattered.

She waited what felt like an aeon but was in reality only seconds and then he smiled, a smile so full of warmth and promise and joy, and she smiled back and then he rose to his feet, held a hand out and pulled her up and straight into his arms.

Then there was no more talking, no more rationalising… There was just the sheer bliss of kissing him, knowing as the need escalated, as he deepened the kiss, that this time she could go further.

Her hands tugged at the bottom of his T-shirt, helped him to pull it over his head and she gave a small gasp, an exhalation of wonder as her hand skimmed over the hard muscle of his chest. She heard the sound of his indrawn breath, felt his hand slip under her shirt, firm against her back, and she gave a shiver of sheer unbridled pleasure and then soon they were lying entangled on the soft sheets of the bed, lost in the pleasure of each other's bodies, revelling in touch and taste and joy.

CHAPTER TEN

LORENZO OPENED HIS EYES, aware that something had woken him up, aware too of an initial sense of contentment as he registered the silken tickle of Liyana's hair on his chest, recalled the glorious feel of it under his fingers. He was aware too of a sense of connection, of appreciation for her understanding and a happiness that she had trusted him. With so much.

But as he lay there the contentment began to sap, to abate, replaced by a growing sense of unease. And then he realised what had woken him. The rain had stopped. The wind no longer howled. And for a second a sense of loss touched him, a knowledge that this small bubble of time granted by the forces of nature or the hand of fate was over. And he felt a fierce sense of denial, rejection, wanted things to be different. But they weren't.

Speaking with Liyana had been cathartic in a lot of ways but it had also shown him something. Love was a mystery; did his mother love Matt and vice versa or were they caught in a trap, a dependency they couldn't break free of? Had Liyana loved Gregor at the start? How did you distinguish attraction, romance, words from love, reality from illusion? Yet he still didn't want this moment now to end. Was it possible, was there some way it didn't have to? The answer starkly obvious. There was no possible future for them. Because he had nothing to offer Liyana. That was something else that was clear from their conversation.

He was the product of a dysfunctional family, a man who had achieved material success but in truth he'd trade that all in to have been deemed loveable as a child. But he wasn't loveable and he had no concept or understanding of what that meant. True, Liyana didn't want love, but she did want marriage and children. Commitment. And Lorenzo didn't understand or trust that either.

Were his mum and Matt committed—was that an example of for better or for worse? How would Lorenzo know the rules and boundaries? His mother had prioritised her marriage over her son—was that right? What if he ended up hurting Liyana? Plus, he didn't want children. He wasn't cut out by nurture or nature for that precious responsibility.

So there was no future. Her plan was to marry a prince. These last hours needed to remain a secret never to be told, a bubble, a treasured memory. Yet the idea that this was it still hurt and he waited another heartbeat before he placed a gentle hand on her shoulder, watched as she opened her eyes and gave him a sleepy smile. And he knew he would hold that image of her smile, her beauty.

Then her eyes widened as she too registered the sound of silence from outside.

'The storm's over,' she said. Within seconds she had scrambled out of bed and he followed suit. Glanced at his watch and saw that it was early morning. Dawn would be breaking outside.

'We need to make sure we leave absolutely nothing behind.' They were both ready now and Liyana's voice was clinical, held a panic and he knew why. The last thing she needed was history to repeat, for a scandal to brew. They didn't know when the storm had stopped, if even now there were people looking for them.

He made his voice businesslike and reassuring. 'Agreed. With luck we can get out of here without being seen. I'll leave a cash payment.'

Their luck held and once they were outside, they both looked round at the storm-ravaged landscape. There were fallen palm trees, debris and litter but above them the sky was cloud-free, pink tendrils tinging the dawn, the air still and sultry, holding the promise of warmth and sunlight.

'If you couldn't see the consequences, you'd never believe there was a storm,' she said. 'It's as though it never happened.'

'Is that the same for us?' he asked, knowing the answer but asking anyway, perhaps holding onto one last vestige of impossible hope. 'Are we going to pretend it never happened?'

She stopped, turned to him. 'What else can we do?' she asked. Her tone held sadness but also a hard edge of reason and also worry. Perhaps a fear of imminent consequences or a fear he would make things difficult. Not this time. This time he wouldn't let anything taint the magic of the night before.

'I don't know,' he said. 'But I will do whatever you want, handle this however you want to handle it. I just want you to know that I have no regrets.'

'Neither do I.' She paused and smiled at

him, a smile that caught his heart. 'I will hold the memory and treasure it.' She started to walk again, gathered up her hair, deftly wound it up and inserted pins; he could almost see her putting herself back together, shaping her princess persona.

'But it has to remain a secret and everything between us—it has to end now. Because there is no other choice.' Her voice caught and he wondered if perhaps she felt as bereft, as raw as he did. 'If last night gets out the scandal will be unstoppable and I will lose my chance to redeem myself.'

Lorenzo looked at her. 'You have nothing to redeem, Liyana.'

'It feels to me like I do. Speaking to you, reliving my marriage, it has made me see all the points where perhaps I could have, maybe should have done something. But events got out of control. I won't make the same mistake again. This has to stop here. Before… Before it becomes too difficult to stop.' A tear sparkled in the corner of her eye and she blinked fiercely. But too late. He watched it trickle down her cheek and gently, oh-so gently he reached out and caught it, felt her shiver in response.

'It's OK,' he said. 'Please don't cry. I understand and I promise not to make things difficult or complicated for you.' Because she was right. This had to stop here. The scandal would ruin her, and he might well lose Ashan's friendship. Ashan wouldn't understand or approve of his best friend and his sister having a one-night stand. Of course he wouldn't and in truth it was doubtful he would approve even if they were to opt for a relationship. Ashan was heir to the throne of Carathi and he would prefer his sister to ally with a royal prince who could bring real benefit to Carathi. Ashan was also well aware that Lorenzo was not really relationship material, wouldn't want his sister to risk getting hurt. 'But I am glad that we had last night.'

She nodded and then almost abruptly she turned away, pulled out her phone.

'Power is back. I'll call for the boat. I think we just need to say we found a deserted hut to shelter in. With luck no one will be any the wiser.'

And that day and over the next weeks their luck held; they made it back to the ferry port where the boat was waiting for them, returned to the capital and to her relief, due to the focus on assessing the storm's damage, not many questions were asked of Liyana.

She was further relieved that despite its severity the storm seemed to have hit the least populated areas of Carathi the most. There had been no casualties and only minor injuries. More luck.

Yet somehow on a personal note Liyana didn't feel lucky, even though she knew she was. Even though she still gloried in the memory of her time with Lorenzo, she missed him. True to their agreement they had kept contact over the past two weeks to a minimum. She had seen him only twice, once briefly with Ashan and next at a meeting with the minister.

Other than that, she had spoken with him; he was getting on with the practicalities of arranging the ceremony and had kept her informed as to progress. A house had been hired, a date set and soon enough after that Lorenzo would be gone. Would return to his life.

And she would need to make a decision about Prince Luis, would get on with her life.

Liyana closed her eyes, wondered why the idea felt so flat, so dull, so empty. Told herself it would be fine once Lorenzo actually left. And then, yes, he would be back for the public ceremony in two months' time but by then she would be cured of this ridiculous, dangerous urge to throw caution to the wind and arrange to meet him. Come up with some excuse or reason. Too risky.

Sometimes she wondered if Lorenzo was feeling how she felt, or was he already over it? Had he already delegated it to the status of a one-night stand to be forgotten? If not, why hadn't he tried to see her again? Why hadn't he come up with an excuse for them to meet?

Liyana closed her eyes, knew she was being uncharacteristically irrational—Lorenzo was doing as she had asked. She opened her eyes, told herself to focus. She was meeting with Ashan and Kaveesha, a final meeting to go over the plans for the ceremony the next day.

Right on time she heard the ring of the doorbell, went to open the door and smiled a welcome. 'Come in. I've made jasmine tea and Rosa has made biscuits.'

Once they were seated Liyana studied her sister-in-law-to-be, saw the pallor, the dark circles under her eyes. 'Are you OK, Kaveesha? Have you still not thrown off that bug?'

'I'm fine. Just feeling a little queasy. I'm sorry. It's the smell of the tea.' With that Kaveesha rose to her feet. 'Excuse me.'

Liyana frowned, turned to Ashan. 'I'm sorry. I thought jasmine was her favourite.'

'Don't worry about it.' Ashan stood up abruptly, moved round the room picking up ornaments and putting them back and Liyana could sense his jumpiness.

'Is everything all right?'

'Yes. Fine.'

Liyana frowned, knew that, whatever was happening, Ashan was not going to elaborate further. 'I'll get rid of the tea.'

She headed to move the tea tray. And as she did so, the scent wafted up and her own tummy gave a sudden lurch.

Ashan moved towards her. 'Lili, are you OK?'

'I'm fine. Maybe I've caught whatever Kaveesha has.'

As she said the words she was looking straight at Ashan and she saw his expression, almost rueful. 'Bit un—' Her brother broke off and Liyana frowned.

'A bit un what?' she asked.

'A bit unlucky,' Ashan said quickly. Too quickly. 'At least, I don't mean that exactly.'

An inkling of a suspicion crossed Liyana's mind just as Kaveesha returned to the room, looking even paler, and as she looked at Kaveesha closely, her mind whirred, coming up with ideas, scenarios, possibilities. And hot on the heels of those suspicions came a realisation, a sudden sense of foreboding, a darting, nagging worry. Somehow, she got through the rest of the conversation, finalising the logistics of the following day. But all the while her mind was calculating dates, until finally she waved Ashan and Kaveesha goodbye and headed straight upstairs. Checked her calendar and then opened her bathroom cabinet. Checked a packet of pills and then sat down on the edge of her bath and told herself not to panic. Even as panic swirled and roiled inside her.

A panic that continued to spin and tornado the following day as she got ready for Ashan and Kaveesha's ceremony. As she pulled the clothes on, she forced herself to do everything as usual, to make sure there wasn't a hair out of place, to double-check the clothes she'd chosen didn't give any hint of where she was going.

But the whole time her brain alternated between dullness and sharp shocks of anxiety. Because now there was no doubt—she'd done the test. Liyana clenched her hands into fists, the idea of telling Lorenzo making her tummy clench. He didn't want to be a father and she understood why, respected that decision. But now…now he would have no choice and the thought of his reaction added to the panic. The realisation of what she'd done a leaden weight on her chest.

Enough. She would not think about this now. This was a special day for Ashan and Kaveesha, and she would not let this impact their happiness. She gazed in the mirror, forced her expression to one of serenity; today she would be Princess Liyana, Prince Ashan's sister.

And she managed exactly that as she greeted Ashan and Kaveesha at the dock and they made the ferry journey, disembarked and made their way to the house Lorenzo had hired.

It was only when she saw Lorenzo that she faltered; her heart skipped, hopped, jumped and she had to quell the urge to run towards him. Wanted to share the news, tell him that they had created a baby, their baby. For a crazy moment her brain conjured up a delusion where Lorenzo would be happy, would place his hand on her stomach, they would sit together, his arm around her, her head on his shoulder, sit and revel in awe and wonder and joy, sit and plan for a future.

Liyana blinked, banished the ridiculous images and stepped forward as she caught the note of concern in his dark blue eyes. Concern, a question, but also surely a glint of quickly concealed happiness as they gazed at each other.

'All ready?' she asked, kept her voice even, kept her expression dialled to princess mode.

He nodded. 'The celebrant is already here. So we can go straight ahead.' He led the way to the back garden of the house and now Liyana did forget her anxieties, the loom of a future she couldn't even begin to work out. Because Lorenzo had transformed the garden into a true wedding bower, complete with the traditional wooden platform, garlanded in flowers, that basked in the morning sunshine. And now it was time for her to do her bit and as she moved forward to give her reading she felt a rush of joy for the couple.

Liyana read the words she'd written, a brief description of how they had met, went on to say 'I am so happy for you both, so happy that you are committed to each other, committed to spending the rest of your lives together in a union that brings you both happiness and joy. Happy that you found this love.'

Then it was the couple's turn to exchange vows they had written.

Liyana stepped back, stood next to Lorenzo, tried to brace herself at his familiar warmth, the woodsy scent, the sheer reassuring, wonderful bulk of him. Made sure she kept her distance, knew she had to hold it together. But she wanted to enjoy this moment standing so close to him before she turned his world further upside down.

'That was beautiful,' he whispered.

She watched as Ashan took Kaveesha's hands in his. 'We started this journey already committed to a path of duty, a path where we will one day take on the responsibility of ruling and governing a country that I already love and you are growing to love. But along the way something joyous and joyful happened and from duty grew love, a love that will carry and guide us through the ups and downs of marriage, a love that will endure and last.'

Kaveesha looked up at Ashan and Liyana could see love shining in her eyes.

'You have changed my life, Ashan. I always knew you would make a good husband but I never ever dared to believe love could be possible for me. All my life I knew that romance and love were not for a princess. But now… now the world looks different, brighter and better because of our love. A love that blossomed where it was least expected, and is all the more valued for that. I love you and I will never take that love for granted throughout our marriage. I will tend and care for it.'

Liyana blinked back tears and stepped forward with Lorenzo to sprinkle the flower petals and then hugged the happy couple. 'Congratulations,' she whispered.

As they sat down to the meal Lorenzo had prepared, Ashan raised a glass. 'To both of you. Lorenzo and Liyana. Thank you so much. This meant the world to us.' Kaveesha and Ashan exchanged a glance and then Ashan placed his glass down carefully.

'Liyana, I think you may suspect, but we want to share something with you both. Kaveesha is pregnant and whilst we did want this ceremony for all the reasons we told you, the pregnancy made it more important.'

'We are going to tell our parents the truth, but we wanted to do so once the knot has been tied, when we are already husband and wife.'

'So they are presented with a fait accompli

and they cannot decide to terminate the engagement.'

Kaveesha gave a half-smile. 'My parents are extremely strict,' she explained. 'They would be capable of making some sort of example of me.'

'Our plan is to tell everyone that we got married earlier because we were so in love,' Ashan said. 'Then the public ceremony in two months can be a blessing and of course a public celebration.' He smiled at Lorenzo. 'One that will still require the services of a best man in some capacity.'

'But this way no one need know the baby was actually conceived before wedlock,' Liyana said.

'Exactly. We're sorry we didn't tell you before.'

'That's OK. I completely get that.' And she did. 'A secret is only a secret if you tell nobody.' Rising, she went to hug first Kaveesha and then Ashan. 'I am truly happy for both of you.'

'Thank you.' Ashan and Kaveesha rose to their feet.

'Right. We are going to break the news to the parents now,' Ashan said. 'Thank you again. From the bottom of our hearts.'

And with that they were gone, leaving Liyana and Lorenzo alone, and Liyana felt a lurch of trepidation, knew her world was about to change. She inhaled deeply. 'We need to talk,' she said.

CHAPTER ELEVEN

LORENZO STUDIED LIYANA'S EXPRESSION, aware of a sense of foreboding, one that had started to unfurl from the moment he'd seen her. No, not the moment. The first moment he'd seen her he'd felt a burst of unalloyed happiness, as if an unquenchable thirst had been suddenly quenched. And then he'd remembered Liyana was only there because she had to be, because this was the day of the private wedding ceremony, and the happiness had abated.

Then throughout the day he'd had a sense that something wasn't quite right. He couldn't put a finger on it; he knew her happiness for her brother was genuine, knew how much thought she, they both, had put into the ceremony.

Yet despite the near perfection of her princess façade he knew it was a façade, that there was something on her mind. Now she wanted to talk. Part of him was happy because at least it meant she was here. The past weeks had been oh-so difficult. They had met only twice and both times there had been others present. One meeting with Ashan and Kaveesha. The other a meeting with the minister for tourism; the meeting had been a success but to walk away afterwards had made every muscle in his body ache, scream to turn round and go back.

He'd wanted to talk to Liyana, discuss what had happened, he'd wanted to hold her hand, he'd wanted to kiss her, to tug the pins out of her hair and let it fall loose. He'd wanted to be with her. But he knew how selfish that was. How futile it was to even dream these things. Liyana and he had no future. Her future was with a prince. The idea made Lorenzo want to punch a wall. The anger worse because he knew how misplaced it was. Prince Luis could give Liyana what she wanted. Lorenzo couldn't.

Perhaps that was what Liyana wanted to talk about: her forthcoming engagement to Prince Luis. Or perhaps she simply wanted to say goodbye. The thought caused a sense of bereavement. He looked more closely at her. Saw her pallor, the haunted look in her brown eyes.

'Liyana, has something happened?' Concern touched him and he couldn't help it, he stepped forward, wanting, needing, to offer reassurance.

'I… It's complicated.'

'Come and sit back down.' He poured her some lemonade, had noticed she hadn't eaten or drunk very much at the lunch. She tipped her head up to allow the sun to warm her face and then accepted the glass, sipped and placed it down, picked it up again and put it down, then twisted her hands together, looked away from him towards the wooden platform where the ceremony had been held.

Then she inhaled deeply and turned to him, pressed her hands even closer together, her back ramrod straight. Now her gaze met his. 'I'm pregnant.' Her hands unclenched and clenched again, her gaze unwavering.

Lorenzo felt the ground reel, the air suck from his lungs as his brain took each word and tried to make sense of it, to decipher the syllables that seemed to be trying to rewrite themselves to make a different kind of sense.

'But… I thought…'

'You thought I was on the pill. I am. I was on the pill during my marriage and I stayed on it after because I'd always had difficult periods and staying on the pill made that easier. But I guess over the past months I got a bit less reliable at taking them regularly. I checked the packet and I'd missed a few. I did a test. Two tests, in fact. They are both positive.'

Lorenzo tried to think through the fog of shock, disbelief and surreality. For an instant he wondered if this was how Roberto had felt when he had found out about Lorenzo and Daisy. Perhaps how Matt too had felt. The thought was chased away by the sheer terror; he was going to be a father. He didn't know how. He wouldn't be good enough. And this time it would be worse, because now his short-comings would hurt others. Hurt Liyana. Hurt the baby, the child. His child. Liyana's child. Their child. All the doubts, the fear of a genetic or learnt incapacity to parent, the knowledge that often poor parenting passed from one generation to the next, swirled like a dark cloud around him.

Liyana's voice penetrated the fugue of panic. 'You don't have to worry. I know you don't want the responsibility of a child. I am not expecting anything from you.'

'Not expecting anything?' Lorenzo brain-achingly, finally ground into gear and outrage added to the mix, the vortex of emotions, an outrage so strong he clenched the edge of the table, had to force his voice to stay calm. 'You think I'll walk away from my child. Like Roberto?'

'I…' She faltered slightly and he realised despite himself his voice had held a hard anger. Then she jutted her chin out. 'I don't know what you'll do,' she said. She took a deep breath. 'You are a kind, good, caring person but you have also done me the courtesy of being honest with me. You were clear you didn't want to be a parent.' Her voice softened. 'And I respect that. This is on me. I told you it was safe. I messed up.'

'Is that how you feel about the baby? That we've messed up?'

'No. That's not what I meant. I will love this baby. I just meant I accept he or she is *my* responsibility.'

Lorenzo took a deep breath, identified that through the stormy dark vortex of feelings there was one clear overriding thought. 'I won't walk away from my child.'

Once the words were said a small measure of calm was restored, because he knew them to be true. The terror was still there, the fears and the doubts but, regardless, he acknowledged, 'This baby is our responsibility. We made him or her together.'

He could read scepticism on her face and

he couldn't blame her for it. 'Liyana. I didn't want to be a father. Because…because I was too scared. Scared that I will repeat my father's mistakes, be it Roberto's or Matt's. Scared that I would end up hurting my own child as I was hurt myself. Scared I'd mess it up. It wasn't a risk I was willing to take. And I am still scared. But I know if I walk away because of my fears that will hurt my baby. I cannot fathom how Roberto walked away from Daisy and me. I won't repeat that mistake and I swear to you I will do everything I can not to repeat Matt's.'

He knew he could never belittle or humiliate any child. And if he didn't feel a bond with his child he'd damn well fake it; he might not have chosen to take the risk of being a dad but now the decision had been taken from him, well, now he'd be a good dad or die in the attempt.

She reached out, covered his hand with hers and now he could sense a deep bond, knew that whatever the future held they were bound together in shared love for their baby, their child. 'I know you will be a great father, Lorenzo. I know that with all my heart and if you want to be part of our baby's life, I know that can only be a good thing for him or her.'

They sat for a moment, one he knew he

would remember for ever, the scent of hibiscus, the tang of lemons, the feel of her hand in his. Then gently she pulled her hand away. 'I am glad. Once I've worked it out, I'll let you know what I decide to do, how I decide to handle this.'

He could hear the panic that underlay the manufactured calm of her voice and now he thought, really thought about what this meant for Liyana.

Here he was worrying about lofty ideals and whether he'd cut the mustard as a father. For Liyana, this pregnancy had such far-reaching consequences—the scandal of a royal princess being pregnant out of wedlock would be shattering. There was no good spin, no material that could be woven into an illusion of positivity. She would be a single mother in a country where this was a taboo. Marriage would no longer be possible. Her parents would be furious and, worse, they would be disappointed. And what about Ashan? Lorenzo knew it would end their friendship. Worst of all, how would it affect their child. The illegitimate result of a one-night stand. Would he or she be granted royal status? How would it impact him or her?

The questions resounded through his brain

and he could only imagine what this was doing to Liyana. Because there were no answers or at least no good answers. The strands whirled around his head and as he thought the solution struck him with blinding clarity. There *was* a way to take all of this and weave a solution.

He took her hands in his. 'Marry me,' he said.

Marry me. Marry me. Marry me.

The words hung on the air, danced in the sun-warmed breeze and Liyana wasn't sure whether they were words of salvation or words worthy of a soap opera.

How had she let this happen? She'd been so sure she was in control this time; that fate was giving her another chance to do it right. This night with Lorenzo had been above board: he had known who she was; they had both known the score. Damn it, she'd kept to the rules, accepted they could have only one night. But it had still been too big a risk. She knew basic biology. And she shouldn't have taken even the smallest risk. She should have seen that fate was tricking her. Again. After all, that was how it had started with Gregor. One coffee, one kiss and she'd been propelled into a disaster. Now here she was again.

Though this was different. Lorenzo wasn't promising her love. But he was offering her a way out.

'Marry me,' he repeated. 'You were willing to marry Prince Luis. Why not marry me instead?'

'It's not like that. It's not a game show.'

'I know that.' He started to pace then stopped in front of her. 'I am not suggesting you are the prize, or that I am for that matter.' She heard a slight sadness in his voice, knew that he could never believe that he was a prize. 'I understand your reservations, understand that this is a bit sudden. But I truly believe this is the best course of action. For the baby. How will our child be treated as an illegitimate royal baby?'

Liyana sat down, horrified that this aspect hadn't even occurred to her. All she had thought about was her determination to have this baby, keep this baby, love this baby. Now she imagined the disappointment etched on her parents' faces, how Ashan would react, how it would affect his friendship with Lorenzo, a friendship that she knew was precious to them both. How the people would react, how she would be shunned, no longer taken seriously as a royal advisor.

But now his words stopped her in her tracks. An illegitimate royal baby. That was a scandal of epic proportions, one that would run and run, worse than any generated by her grandfather. Liyana could weather the storm, accept being shunned, but how could she inflict that on her child? She wouldn't bring that on anyone. And Lorenzo was offering her a way out. Offering their child legitimacy, a life of acceptance. But…what about Lorenzo himself?

'You said you didn't want to get married, you didn't want a family. How can I accept your proposal?'

'Because things have changed. What I wanted before is no longer relevant. This baby changes everything. I want to do the right thing for my child.'

She got that: got that he wanted to do what no one had done for him. 'But I am not proposing some sort of sacrifice. I *want* to do this, be part of my child's life. And I think we can make it work. I remember everything you said about an arranged marriage and I think we can build a proper, solid, happy marriage based on liking and respect and attraction. I will do my best to be a good husband and a good father. I know I am not a prince and can't bring Carathi the same benefits, but I can invest in

Carathi and I will do my best to convince your parents that I am not a bad bet. What do you think? Will you marry me?'

Liyana listened, heard the sincerity in his voice and felt a warmth that he would do this for his child. Their child. And a picture formed in her head. Herself and Lorenzo stood together, she was holding a dark-haired baby in her arms and they were both smiling down on the infant with love in their eyes. Fast forward to a happy toddler holding their hands, being swung up in the air. Herself looking up at Lorenzo with love in her eyes. Love for this wonderful, caring man.

Her thoughts ground to a screeching, tearing halt. Love? Please, God, no. She didn't want love. Didn't trust love. She'd thought she loved Gregor and all that had brought her was humiliation and heartbreak.

And that was all this love could bring. Love for a man who would be horrified by the very thought. She remained very still, dropped her gaze down to her hands, hoped, prayed that Lorenzo hadn't clocked anything, that she hadn't somehow given the game away.

This changed everything.

For one last lingering moment she allowed herself to hold the image in her mind, a happy family. A loving family. And then slowly it faded, slipping away from her into the shadowy, elusive realms of never to be. She twisted her hands together, thought instead of real scenes, cold, hard-edged reality. Her own marriage to Gregor, where she had been trapped with a man who didn't love her. She knew Lorenzo would never be unfaithful, but how much worse would it be to be striving every day to win his love, day in, day out, trying to turn respect and liking into the real thing? Working out how to be the perfect wife. Again. The idea unbearable, a slow drip drip of daily torture. And all the time trying to hide her love, hide something that should be open and joyful. Because she knew it would tear Lorenzo in half to be in the position Matt had been in: loved by someone he could not love back.

Now her stomach felt the weight of a cold, hard stone of knowledge that she had to do the right thing, whatever the cost, whatever the scandal. Because this marriage would be wrong. She would be entering it based on a lie. She'd lived a lie since her ill-fated marriage to Gregor; now it had to stop. Even though she knew this would break her heart. And inside her she was aware of a sudden roil and roll of sadness, of a sense of something coming together, something bleak but right, something desolate but necessary.

Clenching her hand around the edge of the wooden table, she looked at Lorenzo, took in the now oh-so familiar features, the deep dark blue eyes, the dark unruly hair, longer now with a slight hint of recalcitrant curl. The firm jaw, the jut of his nose, the character and masculine beauty of his face. And she knew what she had to do.

Lorenzo saw anguish and thought on Liyana's face, realised he was holding his breath as he awaited her response.

'It won't work,' she said, her voice quiet, but he heard a steel edge to it and a sudden sense of loss touched him, even as he told himself that he could change her mind, that this was the best solution. Because it was… They could bring their child up together; they could build on the connection they already had. Work out a framework that would enable their marriage to work.

'Why not?' he asked, striving to keep his voice reasonable. After all, that was what Liyana had said she wanted: a marriage based on niceness, with rules and boundaries.

'For a start, because it is not fair on you. You don't want marriage or commitment.'

'I do want this marriage,' he said evenly. 'I want to be there for our baby. Properly.'

'And you will. We can live half the year on Carathi, half the year somewhere else. You can see our child as much as you want. Every day if you like. We can work that out. You will be there for the baby.'

But she didn't want him to be there for her. The knowledge slammed into him; the rejection sucker-punched him. Liyana didn't want him; he'd known he had nothing to offer her before, but now…now she was rejecting him when he surely did have something to put on the table. The chance for their baby to be in a family, the chance to avoid scandal, the chance to legitimise her baby. Yet all of that wasn't enough to make marriage to him palatable.

For a fleeting moment Lorenzo wondered how this could make sense; Liyana had been the one to propound an arranged marriage, had been on the cusp of marrying a prince in the line of duty, for a family, had professed that sort of marriage would make her happy. But not to him. Shades of his past. Matt had been happy to parent Daisy but not him.

But this was bigger than him.

'What about the effect on the baby if we don't get married?'

'I don't know,' Liyana said quietly. 'I will need to speak to my parents, look at the legalities. If necessary, perhaps we could go through a legal formality, so the baby is legitimate, then get an immediate annulment. If you agree to that. But if that isn't possible then so be it. Because marrying you for duty's sake is wrong. I can't keep running and hiding from my mistakes, making decisions based on how much scandal will be caused.

'I stayed with Gregor for all the wrong reasons, because I didn't have the courage to leave him. I need to find the courage not to marry you for all the wrong reasons. I don't want our child to feel we married because of him or her. We may not have intended the pregnancy but I know we will both love our baby without reservation. *That* is the important thing. But the marriage, the spending the rest of our lives together, that is a step too far. I won't create another trap. For you or for me. You have one life, Lorenzo, and I won't take that away from you.

'Kaveesha said earlier that she had never dared to dream of love. I know you think love is not for you but by marrying me you will lose the opportunity to find out. Even if love isn't for you, marrying me will mean you also lose the opportunity to have the type of relationship you want, that works for you. I won't do that to you because I am too scared of scandal to do what is right.'

Lorenzo heard the certainty in her voice, felt every word, every inflection as a blow, a barrage that he couldn't mount a defence against, a boxer up against the ropes. Because there was no defence. Because her words could be turned, mirrored. By marrying him, Liyana would be giving up *her* life. A life that had already been constrained by rules and regulations, a life that had already held one miserable marriage. And by marrying him Liyana would give up *her* chance to live her life as she wished. Would still be conforming to the rules. This way she would be free, free to find her own way in life.

And she *did* deserve a life where she wasn't ruled by the fear of scandal. A life where she could do what she wanted to do and maybe that would be a life without a relationship. After all, her motivation for marriage had always been to have children. Now she would have a child and maybe Liyana would decide to remain single. But the point was she would have a choice. To live her life as she wanted. To the full.

And perhaps her way would lead to true love. Even if she didn't need it, she deserved it, deserved what Kaveesha had, deserved a man capable of love, who knew how it worked, a man who she could love and would love her back and light her world the way Ashan lit Kaveesha's.

And so, he wouldn't mount a defence. He'd sketched out his hope they would have a future together but what he could offer was not enough. Better to accept that now, better to start parenthood as they meant to go on. Just as he should have accepted that Matt couldn't love him long before he'd given up. He wouldn't distress Liyana, understood that this decision had taken courage.

So he didn't say anything to try to change her mind, simply asked one question.

'Are you sure? Sure that is what you want?'

'I am sure it's what's right. So yes, I am sure.'

'Then it will be as you wish. And, Liyana, I understand and I admire the courage you are showing. Our child will grow up being proud of you, and please know I will support you in every way I can.' The thought of the storm that was about to break over her tightened his chest with a need to protect her and a corresponding pain that she didn't want that from him; didn't want the protection he'd offered. 'Let me come with you to tell your parents, or, if you prefer, I will see them first.'

Liyana shook her head. 'That is truly kind of you, but no. I would prefer to do this myself. I need to do this myself, stand on my own two feet. Later, if need be, you can see them, reassure them that you intend to be a good father, reassure them that you will continue to invest in Carathi.' There was a sadness in her eyes. 'And Ashan…'

'I will tell Ashan.' There was no way he would let Liyana break this news to her brother, his best friend, alone.

'We will tell Ashan together. But let's wait a little while; I want to help him explain his early wedding to my parents and I want…'

'Him to have a chance to be happy for a while,' Lorenzo said and, in that instant, he felt a searing sense of regret and sorrow that he and Liyana had no chance of happiness together. Along with a secondary sense of loss that he would lose Ashan's friendship, that he would lose the one person who liked him for himself.

She nodded. 'We can sort out any other details another day. Thank you, Lorenzo. For everything. For being my knight in shining armour, for offering to come to the rescue. But now it's time I face my own battles.'

She rose to her feet, reached out and touched his arm gently and there it was still, the sense of connection. A connection that needed to change. Their connection now would be their child. And with that she headed for the door and he knew that, although of course he would see her again, somehow it could never, would never, be the same.

Three days later

Liyana sat, staring at her computer screen, unsure why she even had it on. There was no possibility of doing any work, not when she was due to see her parents in the next hour. They wanted to discuss Prince Luis. The thought almost risible. Because even if there were no baby, she could never have contemplated that marriage. Wouldn't marry one man when her heart belonged irredeemably to another.

She hadn't planned on telling her parents the truth just yet but now she would have no choice. Her stomach churned at the very idea;

it went beyond the realm of her imagination to even consider her parents' disappointment. At least Ashan was away, visiting Kaveesha's family on the island of Varina. Both sets of parents had been less than happy about the situation but in the end had accepted what was done was done and the official royal wedding celebrations would be a blessing of the marriage. So, Ashan wouldn't be present at the meeting; there was still a little breathing space before he needed to know. Her heart wrenched with a fear that this would destroy his friendship with Lorenzo. She touched her tummy gently. 'We won't let that happen,' she whispered.

But all those emotions, the strum of nerves, the sense of guilt, were nothing compared to the bleak sense of desolation, of emptiness, the ache of missing Lorenzo that she carried with her every waking minute. It was no use telling herself she would still see him, that they would co-parent. That simply made the pain worse when she remembered what she had given up. The chance to live with him, be with him, marry him.

Knowing her decision was correct didn't help. She couldn't marry him when she loved him and he didn't love her back. She closed her eyes and memories assailed her—the intent look in Lorenzo's dark blue eyes when he listened to her, the way his face creased when he smiled, the way he'd held her, the beat of his heart as she'd slept nestled on his chest.

'Lili.'

She opened her eyes, realised to her horror that there was a tear trickling down her cheek and, even worse, Ashan was standing in front of her.

'I thought you were visiting Kaveesha's family,' she said, trying to keep panic from her voice, her brain racing to factor his presence in.

'I was. I came back. To see Lorenzo before he went to London. I wanted to thank him in person for everything he did for Kaveesha and me.'

'Oh.' Liyana tried to read her brother's expression. Surely Lorenzo wouldn't have betrayed her trust by telling him without her, even if he had done so to try and protect her. She tried to think of something to say. 'How was he?' she managed, aware that her voice held a tremor. Aware that she wanted to know. Was Lorenzo feeling even a little bit upset, feeling a fraction of the devastation that raged inside her?

'I don't know,' Ashan said. 'That's why I've come here.'

'I don't understand.'

'I've known Lorenzo a long time and I know how private he is, how much he keeps to himself, but if I had to say how he is, I would say he is ravaged by something. That he is struggling with something that even he can't fully mask, though he made a damn good try. I wondered if you had any idea what is going on?'

'I…' Her heart clenched at the thought of Lorenzo having to speak with Ashan, knowing what he knew and unable to tell him the truth. Lying to a best friend he felt he'd betrayed.

'Lili, I know something is going on. I could see it in his face and I can see it in yours. I want to help. Let me try.' Ashan thought for a moment. 'If you won't or can't tell me I will go to London. See if he will tell me.'

Liyana made a decision; she wouldn't put Lorenzo through that. In any case, once she had told her parents, now that Ashan was here he would find out anyway.

'I'll tell you,' she said. 'Lorenzo and I were going to tell you together, but I hope he will understand.' She took a deep breath. 'I'm pregnant. With Lorenzo's baby.' In other circumstances Ashan's face would have been comical, but not in this one. Because after shock came anger and she put a hand out swiftly.

'Listen to me, Ashan. I was planning on marrying Prince Luis, to do the right thing, do my duty. Lorenzo and I…he and I…we connected in a way I can't explain.' She couldn't tell her brother she'd fallen in love. Again. Another disaster. 'We both knew it could only be one night. When I found out I was pregnant Lorenzo offered to marry me. He wants to be there for our child. He thought we could build a solid marriage, be a family, be happy together.'

Ashan frowned, sat down opposite her, looked at her for a long time.

'Then why didn't you accept? You were thinking of marrying Prince Luis, who you barely know, for duty. Wouldn't marrying the father of your child for the same reasons be a good idea?'

Liyana looked away, scared her brother would read her expression, work out the truth. 'It wouldn't be right to marry Lorenzo. It would have been a marriage founded on Lorenzo's sacrifice. He isn't royal, he doesn't have to marry for duty.'

'That's true, but…' Ashan frowned. 'Lorenzo wouldn't have offered if he didn't want to do it.'

'I know, and I know he wants to be there for the baby, but that doesn't mean he has to marry me. Marriage isn't that easy.' God knew, she knew that.

Perhaps Ashan was reading her mind.

'I know you don't like to speak about Gregor and maybe I was wrong about him.'

'You weren't wrong.'

'It gives me no pleasure to hear that. But whatever Gregor was, I know Lorenzo is worth a hundred of him. He has honour and he has integrity. I know he has his own baggage, his own demons, but he is a good man. There are no guarantees in life, Liyana, but I am as sure as I can be that Lorenzo would never knowingly hurt you.' He hesitated. 'But I also know that doesn't mean you should marry him.'

Liyana looked at him, knew her surprise must show on her face.

'Before Kaveesha, before we fell in love, I would be telling you to marry him for the sake of Carathi, to avoid scandal. Now I feel differently. I don't believe you should marry him purely for duty's sake. But you said…you felt a connection you can't explain. That's how I felt about Kaveesha. It took me a long while to work out what I felt was love. I don't know how you feel about Lorenzo, maybe you don't either, but think carefully. And if you do love him, don't let your marriage to Gregor, what Gregor did, make you reject that love.'

Liyana sighed, the sense of bleakness intensifying. 'It doesn't matter if I love him or not. Lorenzo doesn't love me.'

'How do you know?'

The simplicity of the question rocked Liyana back.

'And even if he doesn't, he deserves to know how you feel about him. Maybe the only way you can both truly work out the best way forward for you both is to be truthful.' Ashan reached out and covered her hand in his. 'Whatever you decide, I will support that decision.' He rose to his feet. 'And I will go and see our parents. Explain that the marriage with Prince Luis is a non-starter, because you both deserve more than a marriage of duty.' He met her gaze. 'And so do you and Lorenzo.'

'Thank you.' Liyana reached out and squeezed his hand, a surge of love for her brother nigh on overwhelming. 'Truly, and I will think about everything you've said. But before I do I need our parents to know the truth. I will see them myself.'

Once Ashan left Liyana sat, stared out at the patch of garden outside her office, no longer concerned about telling her parents, because Ashan was right. It was important for the truth to be told. She had lived a lie for too long. And it was time to stop. And by concealing her love from Lorenzo she was lying once again. She could tell herself it was to protect Lorenzo but it wasn't only that. It was to protect herself; she was too scared to tell him, scared to risk her heart, risk further humiliation and rejection.

But Lorenzo would never humiliate her and if he couldn't love her then so be it. That wasn't a rejection of her; it was simply a fact she would have to live with. But at least she'd know she'd told him, and at least he'd know he was loved. And it was worth the risk, because Lorenzo was worth the risk. Of course he was…

Lorenzo sat at his desk and forced himself to look over all the paperwork that had accumulated on his absence from the foundation. He'd already spent hours in the boardroom of Take It Away the previous two days and now it was the foundation's turn. He didn't know what else to do but try to immerse himself in his 'normal' life, a futile attempt to pull himself out of the sadness that pervaded his soul, to dull the constant ache of missing Liyana. But his normal life seemed grey, lacking something he'd never known was missing. Lacking Liyana.

And as he looked over a proposal for an activity camp, for funding practical training courses, various fundraisers, instead of words on a screen he saw Liyana's face, her radiant smile, the way her forehead creased, the stray tendrils of hair that framed her face and were impatiently pushed aside if she was busy.

Then there were all the things he wanted to share with her, things that might interest her about the foundation, ideas that could be used on Carathi. But he knew better than to use the excuse to contact her. It was shades of his childhood; he had to accept that what he had offered wasn't enough. He wasn't enough.

There was a perfunctory knock on the open door of his office and he looked up expecting one of the staff to come in. Or one of the teenagers at the centre today.

Instead, it was his sister.

'Hey. I wasn't expecting you today.' Daisy volunteered at the foundation, but Lorenzo was pretty sure she wasn't due in today. 'Is everything OK?'

'That's what I came to ask you. I've barely heard from you in weeks. I wondered how Carathi was.'

Her eyes, a light blue where his were dark, studied his face, no doubt seeing way more than he wanted her to see, a facet of their twinship. Yet he tried to hold his expression to neutral.

'What's wrong?' Daisy said, her voice filled with concern. 'Please don't say nothing, because I know something has happened. The messages you did send sounded odd and you haven't been in contact since you got back and…and I can just tell.'

'It's a bit complicated,' Lorenzo settled for. 'There are some things I need to work out. But in a nutshell…you are going to be an aunt.' Better to focus on the positives, on news that was joyful and something to celebrate. 'But don't tell anyone else yet.'

'Of course I won't.' Daisy grinned at him. 'And that is incredible news. Who is the mum?'

'Princess Liyana.'

There was a moment's silence. 'So when is

the wedding?' Daisy asked instantly. 'I am assuming you are going to marry her.'

'She won't marry me,' Lorenzo said flatly. 'Which I understand.'

Daisy frowned. 'Surely pregnant Carathian princesses need to be married.'

'She doesn't want to marry me because she doesn't think it is right to marry for duty. She wants to be free, to lead her own life and leave me free to live mine. But we will co-parent. I want this baby and I will be there for him or her every step of the way, Daisy. I won't walk away from my child and I will do everything I can to be a good dad.'

'I know that.' Daisy's voice was fervent. 'But there is something else I don't understand. If you're happy about being a father, why are you clearly so miserable? I don't need to be your twin to sense the cloud around you. In fact, I haven't seen you like this since we discovered the truth about Dad.'

'It's not because of the baby. Truly.' It felt really important that Daisy knew that, believed that. Because it was true and he couldn't bear for there to be any doubt about that.

'I believe you. But then why are you miserable?'

It was an excellent question. Liyana had

given him the best of all worlds. His freedom and the chance to parent. Yet he was more miserable than he had ever been,

'Because I wanted to marry Liyana.' The truth slammed into him. 'I want to marry her. And I miss her. And...'

'And?' Daisy prompted.

'And I love her.' It was so damn obvious now he'd said it, and images streamed his mind, of holding Liyana's hand, holding her, laughing with her, cooking for her, dancing with her under the stars, waking up with her cocooned in his arms. The wrenching ache of missing her, the way anything and everything reminded him of her, the desire to share everyday things with her.

Daisy beamed at him. 'That's a good thing,' she said firmly.

'No. It isn't. It's history repeating, shows I haven't learnt.'

'Stop that right there. This isn't about Dad. I don't presume to understand how Dad's mind works and we have long since decided that subject is not one we discuss. But I do know that what he did was wrong.'

'I know. Of course he shouldn't have treated me like that, but the bottom line is he didn't or couldn't love me. The lesson is you can't force love. And Liyana doesn't love me.'

'Do you know that? When you offered to marry her did you mention love?'

'Of course I didn't. I didn't even realise then that I loved her. Even if I had I wouldn't have told her.'

'Why not?'

'Because it wouldn't be fair on her. She made it clear she doesn't want to marry me.'

Daisy shook her head. 'I know I wasn't there, but it sounds as though she made it clear she didn't want to marry you just for the baby's sake. Maybe marrying you for love is something she would consider.'

'But…' Lorenzo's mind reeled, still absorbing the incredible fact that he loved Liyana, the dawning knowledge that this love felt like something to be celebrated, shouted from the rooftops. Yet that joy was tempered by a fear that telling Liyana would make things complicated, that it would lead to hurt, to rejection.

'I get that you're scared, L. I guess love is scary. But you won't know how she feels unless you ask. And unless you are one hundred per cent sure she doesn't love you, you can't know what her answer will be. Is that a risk you want to take with the rest of your life? And hers?'

Another excellent question and his brain raced, his emotions veering from hope to despair as he tried to work out what to do. Recalled Liyana's words, saying she wouldn't marry him for the wrong reasons, wanted him to be free to find love. Well, damn it—he had.

Daisy rose to her feet. 'Promise you'll think about it. Love is a pretty rare thing and if you have true love then don't run away from it because of Dad.'

'I promise. Thank you.'

He hugged his sister, watched as she exited the room, sat back down, his mind whirring. He loved Liyana and Daisy was right. If there was any chance she loved him back, any chance he could win her love, he couldn't walk away from this. Couldn't allow his own fear of rejection to win. Wouldn't let Matt's actions, Matt's behaviour, taint and sully this emotion, this feeling he had for Liyana. And if Liyana really did not, could not, love him, then, yes, he would accept that, but he had to be sure. He took his phone out; he'd sort out a flight back to Carathi for today, charter a jet if need be. Whatever it took.

Before he could do anything, his phone

beeped. He looked down, felt his heart pound as he read it.

Hello. I am in London. Please could we meet?

It was from Liyana and as he noted the venue he wondered what it could mean.

Princess Liyana of Carathi entered the grandiose portals of the discreet yet luxurious London hotel, headed across the black and white marbled floor of the lobby, past the verdant green potted plant. She wondered whether it was the same one she had hidden behind seven years before, realised the random thought was a distraction from the nerves that tumulted in her tummy, strummed notes of anticipation and anxiety.

She entered the bar, scanned the room, aware of the differences and the similarities. There were different pictures on the walls now—rural landscapes had replaced the animal motif. The furniture was similar, though the sofas and chairs were now navy blue and burgundy. Liyana headed towards the same corner sofa, knew she was ridiculously early, knew there was no point expecting Lorenzo for at least fifteen minutes, yet she shifted across the sofa so she could scan the entrance.

Then a man entered the bar and she froze, looked and kept looking, seemingly unable not to. Blinking, she told herself to get a grip. Yet still her entire focus was on the man as he glanced round. He was tall, looked to be about her own age, mid to late twenties. His dark hair was unruly, as though he hadn't had time to cut it, his lithe movements spoke of an easy power, a focused energy. He stood and scanned the room and she could see the tension in his body, the set of his determined jaw.

Then Lorenzo saw her and he smiled, a smile that held relief and a happiness that matched her own, and she wondered if perhaps he had missed her as much as she had missed him.

Hope surged and she pushed it down, aware that the smile could be a trick of the light, that she could be seeing what she wanted to see. He walked towards her and she tried to work out what image to project, aware that for once in her life she couldn't figure it out, and she just waited, suddenly not caring if he could read her expression. See hope, anxiety, happiness at the sheer sight of him. Her body feeling as though she were having a drink after days in the desert.

'Hello,' he said.

'Hello,' she replied. 'I'll get the drinks.'

She returned a few minutes later holding a Kensington for him and a mocktail for herself. They sat for a moment. Part of her wanted to make small talk, prolong this time with him before she came to the crunch, before she risked everything, put her heart on the line; another part wanted to launch herself at him and kiss him and the rest of her simply wanted to blurt out her love, tell him how she felt. Wanted him to know he *was* loved.

'Thank you for meeting me.'

'You're welcome. I'm glad you messaged. I was about to book a flight to Carathi. I wanted to see you.' He paused and she knew she had to speak first, had to say what she needed to say, before she lost her nerve.

'I wanted to see you too. Because I've... well, I've got something I want to tell you.' Damn, she was floundering here. 'Something I want to ask you.'

She sipped the drink, hoped the sour tang of the lemons would kick-start her brain into gear, calm the fluctuating emotion. Then she looked at his face, the strong planes, the dark blue of his eyes, and she knew she could trust this man. That, whatever the outcome of this conversation, he would strive not to hurt her. That he would be honest with her. Would see her and hear her. The real her.

And that knowledge did give her the courage she needed. Reaching into her bag, she brought out a square, flat box and handed it to him.

With a questioning look he opened it. Looked down at the double-banded man's bracelet, the two bands made of woven leather embedded with two silver triangles with their initials on them, a double L.

'It's Carathian tradition,' she explained. 'The bracelet is a symbol of commitment.' She took a deep breath. 'I asked you here because I wanted to tell you that I love you.' She reached across the table, then pulled her hand back. Knew she could not invoke touch, had to keep attraction from the table. 'I want to ask you if you want to share your life with me. Not because of our baby, not because it makes sense, not because it's good for Carathi, not because it avoids scandal. But because I love you.' There. She'd said it.

As she looked at him, she saw shock touch his face and then morph into a smile so full of joy her heart ached. 'And I love you,' he said. Waited a beat as he clasped the bracelet around his wrist and repeated the words as if they filled him with the same happiness exploding inside her. 'I love you. The past few days I have missed you so much it hurt. I have been walking around in a dense black cloud of misery. Now…' His smile widened. 'Now I am so happy it hurts. You have changed my life. You've made me see that the risk of love is more than worth it. I was scared of getting hurt and I was scared of hurting someone else.

'Of course, love comes with that risk, but the other side of it is the joy and happiness it gives, the way my breath catches in my throat when I see you, the way my heart hops, skips and jumps. It is the simple joy of holding your hand, sharing a joke, eating a meal together. It is the light you bring my life. That is love. I was scared of the power it gave but now, now I can see it isn't about one person having power over another. That isn't love. Love is when you want to be there for the other person, to support them, when you work together.'

Liyana could feel happiness bubble up inside her and now she did reach out and cover his hand with hers. 'Exactly. What I had with Gregor was never any of that. It wasn't about being equals, or partners. It wasn't love. What *we* have is love, because I know I will always want to support your ideas and I know you will support mine. I know you will be honest without being hurtful. I know if we have any problems or issues we will work through them. I know I can talk and you will listen. And no one has ever done that before. You have changed me because with you I can truly be myself. Liyana. That is the person you see, that is the person I am with you. No mask, just me. I can just be me.'

'And that's who I love,' he said softly. 'You. I love the way you care about people and your country. I love your curiosity and your knowledge. I love your courage, the way you face up to things, I love your impulsiveness. I love how you have unlocked my ability to love and be loved. I love you. With all my heart and soul.'

'And I love you. I love you for the way you have shaped and forged your life, the fact that you want to give back. I love your determination and your drive and I love your kindness and I love that I know you are going to be an amazing father.'

'And you will be an amazing mother. And together we will be an amazing family. We will be unstoppable.' He raised his glass. 'To us.'

'To us.'

'So what do you want to happen next?' he asked, and she recognised the same question he'd asked seven years before and she grinned at him.

'Honestly?' Her voice was low, husky and he felt the haze of desire thicken.

'Yes.'

'I want to spend the next few hours with you, the first hours of the rest of our life together. I want to have fun. I want to walk the streets of London and go with the flow and see where it takes us. I want to eat ice cream under the stars and after that I want to come back here to the room I have booked.' She smiled at him, hoped he could hear the love in her voice, see it in her eyes. 'And then…'

'Kaboom,' he said. And, leaning over, he kissed her and Liyana knew that fate had brought them full circle and he was her beginning and her end, that their love would bring them both joy and happiness for ever.

EPILOGUE

Carathi, a few weeks later

LIYANA STOOD ON the traditional wooden platform, a platform Lorenzo had made himself for their wedding ceremony. A small quiet ceremony attended only by close family: her parents, his sister, Ashan and Kaveesha. They had decided they would ask his mother and Matt to the wedding blessings that would be carried out at a later date.

Liyana looked around the platform and felt her heart swell with happiness and love. Lorenzo had placed a trellised arch behind it woven with flowers from the market, flowers that were the colour of the Carathi flag, and she knew he wanted to show her that he would respect and love her country. The scent pervaded the air, sweet and light and floral.

Under the trellis he'd put a small shelving unit and on it was a collection of things: glass coasters with pictures of cocktails on them, a printed cocktail menu from the hotel where they had first met and where they had declared their love, a love that made her feel complete. A recipe book of Carathi recipes, a selection of fruit and vegetables from the market, and at the end a photo album embossed in gold lettering, *Our Life Together.*

She looked up at the man she loved, the man she had just promised to spend the rest of her life with. And now it was time to make their personalised vows.

'I love you with all my heart, Lorenzo. You have brought joy and happiness to my life, you have made me a better person and I love you. For the person you are, your caring and kindness, your integrity and honour. I love you.'

His smile warmed, his blue eyes intent and unwavering. 'This day I promise you, Liyana, that I will always love you, I will always respect you and listen to you, be faithful and honest and stand by your side. I offer you my unwavering support and my steadfast loyalty. I offer you my heart.'

Liyana knew she would never forget those vows, the way his deep voice had resonated, his words etched on her heart and soul.

And then they stepped off the platform to

the applause of their families and soon after that they were all standing in the garden, the same garden where Ashan and Kaveesha had held their ceremony.

Liyana smiled as her parents approached them, both smiling though, as always, the King and Queen carried their royalty with them, their dignity and gravitas unmistakeable.

'Liyana, Lorenzo. Congratulations,' her mother said and her father inclined his head.

'This was not what we had envisaged for you, Liyana, but—' and the stress was clear '—we believe you have made a good choice in Lorenzo and we hope and believe that the two of you will be good for Carathi.'

'And good for each other,' the Queen added.

'I meant every word of my vows,' Lorenzo said. 'I will be good for and to your daughter and make it my duty to cherish and protect her. Moreover, I will stand by and support everything I know she wants to do for her country. I hope we make you proud of us.'

'I think you will,' her father said. 'In fact, you already have.'

'So much so,' the Queen said with a beaming smile, 'that we have decided to promote Liyana to the role of Minister of Tourism as she requested. We agree that it is time a woman held a role like this and you have proved yourself already, Liyana.'

As she moved forward to hug her parents, Liyana felt a bonus wave of happiness engulf her.

Liyana watched as her parents then walked away, recalled their reactions when she had told them she would not marry Prince Luis, that she was pregnant, that she had elected single motherhood over a marriage without love.

Her father had been furious, but to her eternal surprise her mother had cut the fury off. Told her father that this was Liyana's right to choose, then turned to Liyana.

'I wish this hadn't happened this way, but your father and I will do our best to support you and we will love our grandchild. You may go now, Liyana, and I will discuss this with your father.' And whatever she had said had worked because her father had sought her out later and reiterated her mother's sentiments.

Of course, both parents had been more than relieved to hear of the marriage, but Liyana would always cherish their initial acceptance.

She turned now as her brother and sister-in-law approached and Liyana smiled as Ashan hugged Lorenzo. Her husband. The thought brought a beam to her face. Her husband and her baby's father. She touched her tummy gently, saw that Kaveesha was doing the same and both women laughed.

Then Ashan glanced across to where Daisy was chatting to the King and Queen. 'I will go and rescue your sister,' he said and after a while Daisy came across to join them.

'Congratulations, both of you. And to the baby too. I can't wait to be Auntie Daisy.'

Her voice was bright but there was a slightly strained cast to her smile and Liyana saw Lorenzo frown. 'You OK?' he asked.

Daisy twisted her little fingers together and Liyana could sense her anxiety. She had got to know Daisy well in the past weeks and she reached out to touch the other woman gently on the arm.

'Shall I leave you two together?'

Daisy shook her head. 'No need. It's just that I've decided to go to Tuscany. I haven't told them yet, but I'm thinking about meeting them.'

'Vittorio and Amara?' Liyana clarified. Lorenzo and Daisy's grandfather and half-sister. Liyana knew that Lorenzo had decided to reach out to them by asking them to Carathi, but was waiting to give Daisy more time to decide what to do.

'Do you want me to come with you?' Lorenzo asked instantly.

'No need,' Daisy said again. 'I think I need to do this myself. I've found a place to stay, on an olive grove, near the Rossi vineyard. Once I get there, I'll see how I feel. Maybe I'll even bump into them by chance. I'll leave it to fate.'

Fate. Liyana looked at Daisy, wondered what fate had in store for her.

Now Daisy's smile looked more natural and she nudged her brother. 'Don't worry. I promise I'll keep you posted and if I need you, I'll call. But for now, you stay with your wife.'

Lorenzo grinned. 'I'll never tire of hearing those words.'

And Liyana knew he wouldn't. They spent the next few hours talking and celebrating until everyone left, leaving them alone in the now starlit garden.

Lorenzo smiled down at her. 'Now, Princess Liyana, my beautiful wife, will you do me the honour of dancing with me?' He walked over to a small old-fashioned CD player that had been under a table and put a CD in.

Liyana's face broke into a smile as she recognised the band—the same one they had listened to at the club, the night before the storm, a night that had been full of frustrated yearning. But now, now she was free to step into his arms as the beat of the drums, the haunting sound of the flute, the notes dancing in the warm night air, created a magical ambiance.

And then his strong arms encircled her and she laid her head against his chest, heard the strong, steady beat of his heart and she felt a tidal wave of happiness, of joy and optimism about her future, their future, about the long and happy marriage that lay ahead of them, a marriage founded on love.

* * * * *

Look out for the next story in
Long-Lost Rossi Siblings trilogy

Coming soon!

And if you enjoyed this story, check out
these other great reads from Nina Milne

The Bride Wore His Convenient Ring
Secret Royal's Napoli Reunion
Their Mauritius Wedding Ruse

All available now!